T0354855

A Watcher Novel

CEDRA WILSON

authorHOUSE®

AuthorHouse™
1663 Liberty Drive
Bloomington, IN 47403
www.authorhouse.com
Phone: 1 (800) 839-8640

© 2019 Cedra Wilson. All rights reserved.

No part of this book may be reproduced, stored in a retrieval system, or
transmitted by any means without the written permission of the author.

Published by AuthorHouse 07/15/2019

ISBN: 978-1-7283-1929-2 (sc)
ISBN: 978-1-7283-1932-2 (e)

Library of Congress Control Number: 2019909960

Print information available on the last page.

Any people depicted in stock imagery provided by Getty Images are models,
and such images are being used for illustrative purposes only.
Certain stock imagery © Getty Images.

This book is printed on acid-free paper.

Because of the dynamic nature of the Internet, any web addresses or links contained in
this book may have changed since publication and may no longer be valid. The views
expressed in this work are solely those of the author and do not necessarily reflect the
views of the publisher, and the publisher hereby disclaims any responsibility for them.

To my loving mother, whose support and compassion allowed my imagination to flourish.

I love you Mommy.

Contents

Prologue

The rain was the best part of living in London. I'm sure most people would disagree—all the gloom and doom and no sun—but in the five years I'd been living here the rain was what had always attracted me. It was also what I was going to miss most.

"Artemis, do you want to talk about this?"

I took my time, getting one last look at the gray sky and the water that splattered the window that I looked out of before turning to look over at my mother, who was driving the car. She had insisted we take one last drive through the country like we often did while we lived here. One last drive was my consolation for getting shipped across an ocean away from my mother.

I took a moment to really look at my mother and, for the first time, I noticed how I didn't look much like her. Mom had a halo of brilliant blonde hair, mirroring her name, Selene, named brilliantly by my grandmother after the goddess of the moon. Mom had passed on her brilliant sapphire eyes to all of her children, but the hair thing got me from time to time. I had inky black hair—supposedly the same as my father, but that's all I knew. Mom didn't like to talk about him and, after a while, I just stopped pushing her.

"Do I really have to move?" I asked quietly, hoping that maybe she'd reconsider sending me away. I couldn't keep the sadness out of my voice; after five years of living in London with my mom, I was being shipped back to New Orleans to live with my sisters, Rhea and Eris.

Mom reached over and took my hand in hers, taking her eyes off the road briefly to look at me and hope that I would see the sincerity in her eyes. "Honey, this is for the best."

"You've been saying that all week." I pulled my hand away from her and crossed my arms over my chest. I could tell that Mom was hurt by what I had done, but I was in too foul a mood to address it. "Ever since you got the job in Dublin and decided out of nowhere that I needed to go back to the States. I want to go to Dublin with you."

"Going to New Orleans to stay with your sisters is what you need right now, not to keep bouncing around the globe with me. You need stability, Artemis, now more than ever."

"You sound like Ray," I mumbled, thinking about my oldest sister who had been the first to jump ship. Mom had been a traveler by nature, moving around every few years when she got restless. Rhea had tired of it and, when she was old enough to go to college, she took off back to the States. Eris left not too long after that, and now they both lived in Mom's hometown of New Orleans, which was to be my new home as well.

Mom chuckled at the comment. "You haven't seen your sisters in a year, and I think the three of you living together again will be a good thing for you."

"All my friends are here," I said in a rather pathetic Hail Mary pass.

"Artemis, you're sixteen. You'll make new friends." She paused for a moment to look in the rearview mirror at some asshole who had sped up behind us and was now riding our bumper down the little country road.

I took a look in the mirror myself and saw the large black Escalade come up fast behind us and continue on our ass. I thought it was off, seeing as most of the roads in Europe were small and compact—a large American car was way too impractical—but I was too stuck on my conversation with Mom to let that oddness occupy my mind for long.

"You say that every time we go," I noted, fiddling with the industrial piercing in my right ear. It was a farewell present from my friends from school when I had told them I was going back stateside. My last act of rebellion had failed to faze my mother, though, seeing as the new piercing had joined the three helix piercings I already had on that ear.

Mom smiled a little. "It's true every time. You and your sisters are going to thank me for this one day."

"Maybe." I leaned against the window, feeling the coolness of it as I closed my eyes. I felt a bump as we started across a bridge and opened my eyes to see the river beneath us, wishing that every second ticking by wasn't a countdown to me leaving my mother behind for God knew how long.

"How about this, once you're settled, I'll come and visit. An entire week, just me, you, and your sisters."

I looked at her and, as much as I wanted to be a bratty teen and just tell her that I never wanted to see her again, I loved my mother too much to let pride come between us like that. I was about to agree to the deal when the crunch of metal on metal met my ears and our car lurched forward. I immediately turned to where the force had come from and saw the Escalade still on our bumper, tapping our car in rapid intervals.

"What the hell?"

"Hold on!" Mom cried out as she white knuckled the steering wheel, trying to keep us on the bridge.

The Escalade was edging over to the side and trying to push our car off the little wooden bridge. Our car was being pushed over to the side and now scraped along the thin side of the bridge.

"Mom!" I screamed, an over-powering realization that we were going off that bridge at any moment sinking in.

Before Mom could respond, the Escalade came up beside us and sideswiped our car. All my ears could register was the crunch of wood and the complete silence that followed as our car fell through the air. Everything happened in slow motion and too fast to react all at once. My brain didn't have time to tell me to scream before our car hit the river in a loud splash, the force hard enough to shoot me forward into the window. After that, all I registered was silence.

"Artemis!" Mom's voice was fuzzy, like I was sleeping and she was trying to wake me and my brain just wouldn't react. "Artemis!"

This time it cut through whatever haze was around my mind. My head was still against the passenger side window where I had hit it upon impact, and pain exploded through the right side the moment I lifted it. I raised my hand to touch it and it came away wet with blood.

"Honey, are you okay?"

I looked over at Mom who was looking over at me with worry all over her face as she cradled her left hand gently, trying to hide it from my eyes, but I could tell it was fractured, probably broken. Her focus was on me, and she didn't want her injury to take away from that.

"I hit my head," I mumbled.

Looking around, my sense of panic rose as I could see our car sinking into the water. It wasn't like in the movies where the car took its sweet time sinking, we were going down fast. We had five minutes at best before we hit the bottom of the river. I couldn't keep the fear out of my voice in that moment as I looked down at my feet that were already submerged in the water that had flooded in from the engine.

"Mom?" I looked over at her and knew she saw the sheer terror on my face.

Mom reached over and put her good arm on my shoulder. "Honey, everything is going to be okay."

I nodded, but I was shaking like a leaf, trying my hardest to take the calm that she had into myself. "What do we do?"

"Roll down your window and swim out, swim to the surface as fast as you can. I'm going to be right behind you." I nodded, grateful more in that moment than any other that Mom had opted to get manual windows and locks when she bought her car. She reached over and kissed my forehead for a long moment. "I love you, Artemis."

I looked at her for a moment, confused by the gesture; I knew the circumstances were rather grim, but it was when she said she loved me that I knew something wrong. There was something she wasn't telling me. I cast the feeling aside, knowing this wasn't the time or place to hash this out.

"I love you too, Mom," I said instead.

I turned my attention to the window and rolled it down all the way, a small bit of panic coming over me as more water flooded the car. Once the window was all the way down, instinct kicked in and I swam out of the car, doing exactly what Mom had told me to do. I swam as fast as I could and didn't stop until I broke the surface of the water.

Gasping for air, I looked around for Mom, remembering she promised she would be right behind me, but she never appeared.

"Mom," I called as terror swept through me. "Mom!"

Chapter 1

"**M**om," I called out, sitting up in bed as I felt my heart jackhammer in my chest. I put my hand over my heart as I struggled to slow it down, taking deep breaths as I remembered that it was just a dream. I was in my bed, not in the water where Mom's car had crashed over a year ago.

When my heart finally reached a semi-normal rate, I went to the bathroom and splashed cold water on my face. The mirror showed how much I had aged in a single year: my long black hair had grown out since I had first arrived in New Orleans, and my blue eyes shone brightly in the crappy bathroom lighting, but there was a shadow behind it. A shadow that few saw and even fewer understood.

I took a long moment before settling myself down, changed into a pair of jogging shorts and a black tank top, and went to into the living room, picking up my bow and arrow before heading into the backyard.

My mother must have known when she named me that I'd have a gift for archery, but then again life is funny that way. Since I was thirteen I had been really into archery, so Mom sprung for lessons while we were living in New Zealand; turns out I was really good at it and became nationally ranked before I turned fifteen.

After the accident I was in rough shape, something that I wouldn't care to admit to anyone, but I allowed archery to be my solace and my only form of coping. Rhea and Eris hadn't understood why I had put all my focus into it, but they had allowed me to grieve my way, and I knew deep down they were grateful that it was a step in the right direction. Eris even set up targets in the backyard for me to practice with—it had been the only way she could get me outside since I had moved in a year ago.

I stepped into the backyard and looked at the sky for a long moment.

It was still mostly a dark mixture of black, navy, and purple, but I could see the traces of gold, orange, and pink breaking as the sun began to rise. The sun had become my morning companion most days; often I was the first one up, but the sun kept me company—I wasn't alone out here.

I took a moment to shake out any traces of fatigue that sleep might still have a hold on, stretching myself out so that I was loose and focused.

I was ready.

Picking up the bow, I pulled an arrow out of the quiver. Loosening my fingers, I pulled back the arrow and took aim at my target on the other side of the yard. I took three deep breaths, keeping my eyes unblinking on the target, and on the third exhale, I released the arrow.

I watched it fly through the air and hit the center with a dull thud. I allowed a small smile to twitch on my face, but I didn't allow the satisfaction to go to my head. Instead, I pulled another arrow out of the quiver and pulled back. I took two deep breaths this time, releasing on the second. I watched the arrow whizz through the air and land a centimeter from the first.

I nodded and knew I was ready. I put the quiver over my shoulder and rolled my neck in a slow circle. I took a long breath and exhaled, shooting the remaining thirteen arrows at the various targets around the yard in rapid of succession. When my quiver was empty, I walked from target to target, collecting the arrows and inspecting my accuracy.

Bullseye.

Every time.

The sun had come out of hiding and risen in the sky by the time the glass sliding door opened and Rhea stepped into the backyard. Since I had moved in, it had become a duty shared between Rhea and Eris to make sure I was still in one piece first thing in the morning. As if in the middle of the night I would fall apart and they would need to put me back together.

Maybe there was some truth to that.

As Rhea came outside, a thought wandered into my mind if she and Eris checked the backyard before they checked my bedroom. After I had moved in, my nightmares about the accident were a lot worse and a lot more recurring than were now, to the point where Rhea and Eris developed the habit of checking on me periodically throughout the night. After about few months the checks got farther and farther apart, but someone always came to check on me first thing in the morning.

I looked at my oldest sister as she stood barefoot in the backyard wearing shorts, a tank top and an overly large sweater. She stood watching me with her arms crossed, her black hair in a messy bun and the shine of her blue eyes dulled behind a pair of black rimmed glasses.

"Nightmares again?" she asked as I lined up my next shot.

I had lost count of how many times I had emptied my quiver of arrows into the targets and circled around the yard, collecting them before starting again. It was a calming routine for me.

I didn't answer her right away, choosing instead to finish what I was doing, taking a deep breath before emptying my quiver on the targets in a different pattern than the last time. I looked over at Rhea who waited calmly for me to answer. "What do you think?"

"Do you want to talk about it?" Rhea and Eris had developed a lot of patience with me over the year; they never pushed me to talk until I was ready, but they were still concerned about my well-being and the questions were always asked . . . even if they weren't always answered.

I looked at her with a blank expression. "Do I ever?"

I loved my sisters and knew they meant well, but there were things I hadn't come around to talking about just yet. Rhea and Eris knew about the accident, but I had never talked to either about it. I wasn't there yet. Rhea made her presence known so I knew I was supported, and Eris had become my shoulder to cry on, even if I wouldn't talk about why I cried. My sisters were my support system, and I knew that without them I would have fallen apart a long time ago.

She pushed her hand through her hair, a tell that she was worried about me. "How long have you been out here?"

I shrugged. "Maybe an hour." I hadn't bothered looking at a clock since I had woken up, and telling Rhea that I had woken up before the sun wouldn't have helped her worry any.

"It's 6:30 now," she said calmly. "Come on inside and get ready or you'll be late for school."

I paused for a moment, remembering that it was my first day back at school since all of this happened. "Can we discuss homeschooling again?" Rhea and Eris had homeschooled me last year while I recovered, but Rhea felt that it was time for me to immerse myself in the world again and be around kids my own age.

I was against this plan in the fullest.

"Artemis Jolie Taylor," Rhea said firmly.

We looked at each other for a long moment, neither one of use wanting to back down. I conceded first, shouldering my bow and heading back inside to get ready for school. I knew Rhea needed this win. She needed to know I was okay and ready to be in the real world with real people again. The thing was . . . I didn't think I was okay.

After I took a shower and got dressed, I came down to find Eris going full Martha Stewart in the kitchen. Since Mom's death, everyone had found their own way of coping. I had my archery, Rhea had thrown herself into work at the store, and Eris . . . Eris cooked.

"Holy crap, Eris." I sat at the island bar in the middle of the kitchen as she moved around like her ass was on fire. "You realize that it's just three of us, right? No one is going to eat all of this."

"Sorry," Eris said as she set a plate of bacon, eggs, sausage, French toast, and waffles in front of me with a glass of orange juice. "I'm just nervous."

Her blonde hair was loose and flew around her head like a small overhead glow. Eris was the only one of us that was a natural blonde like Mom, while Rhea and I both had dark hair that had come from our father. In moments when I wasn't paying attention, Eris looked like Mom and, in those moments, I would forget about what happened for just a second. Deep down, I did really love the moments when I thought that Mom was still alive, but my heart would break all over again when they ended.

"You're not the one that has to go back to high school Eris." I opted for the juice rather than the overabundance of food on the plate. I wasn't very hungry as it was, and my nerves had killed any remaining trace of hunger I had left.

"You should still eat," she said, noticing I hadn't touched the plate.

"I'm not hungry."

Eris had taken over the mothering role since I moved in, always cooking and making sure I was eating, but there was only so much food I could force-feed myself before I felt like I was going to hurl.

Eris held out an apple in compromise and I took it, conceding the fight that had happened quite a few times. Eris cracked a smile at her victory as she put a canvas bag on the table in front of me. "I packed you some beef jerky, protein bars, and some sweets if you get hungry later. This will get you through the school day."

"Eris," I said softly.

"Please," Eris interrupted, knowing she was being overbearing right now but also knowing she was fully within her right. "This way I don't have to worry about you all day."

"Thanks, Eris." I accepted the food, knowing my sisters were more worried than I was about today and they both needed wins.

Rhea came into the kitchen and went straight to the coffee pot before she noticed the buffet Eris had cooked this morning. "Jesus Eris, there are only three of us here."

Eris rolled her eyes and picked up a piece of French toast. "On that note, I will be on the porch, people watching while you two gang up on me behind my back."

Ray and I chuckled as Eris walked out of the kitchen. Eris had always been the dramatic one and, over the years, she had taken it with a sense of humor.

My eyes shifted up to Rhea as she came around the island and leaned directly in front of me, a serious look on her face. "I have something for you." She slid a black box in front of me before picking up a piece of French toast off my plate.

I looked up at her before opening the box. Inside was a pair of stainless steel throwing knives. I picked one up, testing the weight and the sharpness of the blade. Archery had been my first love, but it had also been the gateway for my love of weapons. Over the years travelling, I had trained with various weapons and in several forms of martial arts. Mom thought it was a good way for me to meet kids my own age with the benefit that I could defended myself wherever I was. Rhea and Eris knew this too and, despite the concerns they had over my interest in deadly weapons at such a young age, I knew they also took a bit of relief that I could defend myself when they weren't around.

"You know in normal families, this would be a huge red flag." I smirked as I admired the beauty of the blade.

Rhea eyed me for a moment. "Since when have we been considered normal?" There was a darkness in her humor that I had never heard before.

"True."

"Think of it as a back-to-school gift, a safety blanket since you can't carry that bow and arrow with you."

I looked at Rhea for a moment and saw something in her eyes, a deep worry that I rarely see. Something that concerned me but I couldn't quite place. "You know that they caught him, right? They caught that psycho that ran Mom and me off the road. He's locked up Ray, you don't have to worry."

"Still," Rhea said, smiling slightly to try and ease my concern, "I'd rather be paranoid at this point."

I didn't say anything more at that, instead I took the knives and put them into my school bag. "You're overreacting, Ray, and I don't want you to worry over it."

Rhea leaned forward and kissed me on the forehead. "Hurry up or you'll miss your bus."

Rhea's done, and that told me we weren't going to have this conversation right now. "Fine," I said, willing to give up the conversation for the moment.

"Eris and I will both be at the store today. We'll be back before five. You can call either of us at the store if you need anything. Okay?"

I knew she was talking about my panic attacks. The cherry on top of the traumatized teen sundae was that not only had I come back to my sisters catatonic and dead to the world, but that my night terrors were coupled with severe panic attacks during the day. They had gotten better as I started to pull myself up and with the help of medication, but they did still happen.

I smiled and gave her a little salute, trying to give her the impression that she didn't need to worry about me the way she did. "Aye, aye."

I got my stuff and headed for the door, and had almost made it out before Rhea called after me. "Artemis." I paused with my hand on the doorknob. She was dead serious as she spoke a single word. "Behave."

Rhea knew I had issues in school, from just cutting class to getting into fights on campus—something that had gotten me tossed from a fair share of schools as I bounced around the globe with Mom.

"I make no promises." I smiled and gave her a little wink before I left the house.

Just before I closed the door I could hear Rhea call behind me with more of her new-found dark humor. "You never do."

I closed the door and saw Eris standing on the porch. She was leaning against the railing facing the house next door. I looked over and noticed the house that had been vacant since I moved in last year now had movers going in with boxes. I saw a taller, older guy in his late twenties, probably around Rhea's age, directing the movers as they carried the stuff off the truck.

"Looks like we've got new neighbors." I went to stand next to her.

"Hmm."

I looked over at her and saw she wasn't looking at the movers but up at the sky. She stared up at the clear blue sky, eyes transfixed and unblinking as she did so. Her eyes seemed different, cloudy, as if a storm were brewing in them.

"Eris? What are you looking at?"

Eris blinked for a couple of seconds before she looked at me. "Sorry, guess I zoned out for a minute there." Any other day I would have chalked it up to Eris's spacey nature, but something seemed different. I looked into her eyes and saw the storm behind them was now gone. "Did Rhea give you your back-to-school present?"

"Yep, sending an armed teenage girl to public school, score for the home environment."

Eris chuckled and played with the silver locket that hung around her neck. She brought it to her lips and pressed it to them in a quick kiss. She took off the necklace and looked at me with a smile and an emotion that I couldn't quite place. She placed it around my neck. I looked at the locket and back at her. "There," she smiled, "that way you have something from both of us."

"I remember this." The locket was a family heirloom gifted to the youngest daughter on her sixteenth birthday. No one had any idea why, but it was something fun that Rhea and Eris and I had looked forward to when we were younger.

My finger ran along the outside of the locket, tracing the pentagram design on the front which always made me wonder just how far back the locket went. I opened it and saw a picture of Mom sitting in a rocking chair with a small baby in her arms with two girls standing on either side of her as they smiled happily.

"That picture was taken right after you were born," Eris explained. "I was going to give it back to Mom when I left for New Orleans, but she insisted that I kept it until I saw you again. Said it would bring me protection until I could give it to you."

"That was Mom," I said evenly. "Cryptic until then end. Thank you for this, Eris."

Eris leaned in and kissed me on the forehead. "Have a good day at school, little bird."

Chapter 2

High school was high school, no matter how long you've been out of it. The moment I set foot on campus it was like no time had passed and, for a beautifully fleeting moment, it felt like it used to with Mom, being dropped at a new school in a new town, not knowing a single person and taking a small satisfaction in that. I also took a small bit of comfort that all high schools looked the same; no matter where I went it was the same bright white walls and whiter floor that seemed to glow under the endless florescent light lining the hall.

I took my time as I walked the halls, looking at the black painted lockers in search of the one I'd been assigned. I made sure not to draw attention that I was new, so I walked slowly so I could see the room numbers and signs without looking lost, and made sure not to carry my schedule with me or ask for directions.

I finally found my locker and opened it, making it look like I had some reason to be there. I didn't want to be the first one to class, mostly because I just thought it was awkward being the new kid alone in classroom with a teacher.

After a long moment, I closed my locker door, jumping when I saw a guy appear from behind the door. "Christ, what is your damage?"

He simply laughed as he leaned against the closed doors looking at me. He was tall, like well over six foot, had a muscular build which made it safe to presume that he was a well-known jock, probably a senior. He ruffled his short blond hair, his brown eyes glinting under the harsh hallway lights. "I'm Caleb." He offered me his hand.

"I'm uninterested." My mind subconsciously thought about the knives within reach in my bag.

He laughed again. "I haven't seen you around her before. You new?"

"I'm not sure how that concerns you in anyway, Caleb."

"It doesn't." He hesitated. "I just thought that I had already made note of all the beautiful girls in this school. I guess I'll have to make another note."

I couldn't help but smile at that. I had been hit on before by many a guy in many a language and in many an accent—I wasn't naïve and I wasn't stupid—but it was nice to flirt with a guy again, it made things seem normal for a while.

"So, do you live up to your namesake?"

I looked at him, puzzled. "What are you talking about?"

"You're Artemis Taylor, right?"

I paused at that, ready to take this guy down in an instant if he tried to come at me. "How do you know my name?"

"The archery coach, Coach Spencer, is all worked up over having a nationally ranked archer going to school here."

"You have an archery team?"

"We have a lot of teams around here."

"What makes you think that I would want to join a team and be a jock?"

I heard his rumble of a chuckle. "Jocks get to go to the best parties."

I raised my eyebrow. "What makes you think that I want to even go to parties? Maybe I'm just a good girl that stays home at night and studies until bedtime."

"You look like you know how to have a good time." Caleb gave a cocky smirk. "You don't look like the kind of girl to lock herself in the house while there's fun out there to be had."

"I just might surprise you."

"Well, just in case you don't, I'll be around." The bell rang and the halls started to empty as everyone went to class. Caleb gave me one last smile and a wink before I made my way past him to class. "Let me know when you want to have some fun."

I managed to make it through my first couple of classes under the radar. I was good at it—I kept quiet, sat in the back and made sure I wouldn't have a look on my face that would make the teachers want to single me out in front of the class. Not that these teachers were going above and beyond, so long as I kept my head down and mouth in check, I'd be fine.

Third period was US History, which must have been a last-minute addition to the schedule since it was being taught in a science lab for some reason. I waited until the classroom had filled up before I made my last-minute walk to the only empty table in the back of the room.

The teacher, a stout and balding man in his late forties to early fifties, stood in front of us in an ill-fitting tweed suit and large glasses. "Good morning class, my name is Mr. Black and I will be your teacher for AP US History this year. I will waste no time in jumping into the curriculum for the year. We'll start with the Mayflower and the Pilgrims landing in Plymouth."

The door opened slowly and Mr. Black didn't break stride on what he was writing as he spoke. "You are late. Tardiness will not be tolerated in this class."

"Sorry," the student said as he stepped fully into the room. He was tall and muscular with shaggy brown hair that fell into his eyes. He held up a yellow piece of paper that I recognized as the sheet they gave new students for their first day. "I got lost."

Mr. Black looked at him for a fracture of a second with extreme disinterest. "Don't make a habit of it, young man. Please have a seat. Any empty one will do."

The new kid brushed off Mr. Black's disinterest quickly and made his way to the only empty seat left in the room.

The one next to me.

I made myself interested in the notes I was taking from Mr. Black's droning voice as the new kid sat next to me. He didn't say anything and I didn't know if he had looked at me at all when he sat down. I just wanted to be invisible.

After about twenty minutes I had to force myself to pick my head up and sit up properly as my back started to kink and hurt from sitting slumped over the whole morning. Out of the corner of my eye I could see the new kid staring in my direction. I figured it was better to get this out of the way now rather than three months down the line. I turned to say something but noticed he wasn't looking at me, his gaze fell to my right arm, to the large scar on my wrist.

In a moment of anger and embarrassment, I yanked my arm off the table and placed it out of sight and into my lap.

Our eyes met for a brief moment and I could tell he was embarrassed at staring. "Sorry," he muttered quietly and I could hear the thick Irish accent on his words.

I didn't say anything as I felt my cheeks heat. While being homeschooled, I didn't have to worry about Rhea or Eris staring at my scar. I guess I had gotten used to that so much that I had forgotten to hide it.

So much for being invisible.

I hated lunch on the first day of school. The table seating was drawn like battle lines and everyone who didn't know the right person struggled to find neutral territory to eat. I didn't eat lunch, in fact I wasn't really a three-square meals kind of an eater so much as a preferring to periodically snack throughout the day, accommodated by Eris's bag of snacks.

I hid out in the bathroom for the first five minutes of lunch so that by the time I got to the lunch hall everyone was already seated and I could find my spot without stepping on any toes. I was at least trying to behave for my sisters' sake; I doubted either one of them wanted to be called up to the school after behind told that I had gotten into a fight on my first day.

I spotted a mostly empty table in the corner by the windows and lo and behold sitting at the same table was the new kid from history. We didn't really know each other, but since we had a class together I figured that us sitting together wouldn't be too out there.

The new kid was sitting with his head buried in a copy of *Wuthering Heights*. He wasn't eating lunch, in fact he wasn't paying attention to much of anything going on around him.

"Is it any good?" I asked as I took the seat across from him.

He looked over the top of the book at me for a long moment before putting the book down, opting to indulge my attempt at conversation. His hair wasn't in his eyes anymore and I could see they were the most beautiful toffee color. "You haven't been to Porter's English class, have you?"

I smirked and pulled out my own copy of the book Mrs. Porter had assigned to everyone in her senior English class the moment we walked through the door. "Guilty. I just don't have the motivation to do homework at school."

"It's not homework if you do it at school." He paused for a moment, looking in front of me as I pulled out some beef jerky from my bag. "Not a fan of the cafeteria food?"

I took a bite and shook my head. "I'm not really a meal eater, I'm more of a snacker. What about you?" I motioned toward the empty spot in front of him.

"I live with my brother," he explained, "he isn't big on packing lunches."

I smirked, thinking about Eris's concern over my eating habits. "You want something?"

"What else you got in there, Mary Poppins?"

"Uh, you want a Luna Bar?"

He wrinkled his forehead as if I'd asked him to do algebra in Portuguese. "What the hell is a Luna Bar?"

I chuckled and pulled out a box of Pocky, offering him one.

"I think you just became my favorite person." He smiled, taking one.

Before I thought better of it, I held out my hand out to him. "I'm Artemis."

"Rhode." Rhode took my hand in his.

I took a Pocky for myself, sitting back in my seat as I watched Rhode watching me. "So, why are you being nice to me?"

I shrugged. "I don't have any friends and you don't seem to have any friends, so I figured that misery loves company."

Rhode looked at me for a moment as if trying to analyze whether I was a threat. "You're weird," he said, his mouth turning up at the corners. "I like it."

I winked at him as I took another bit of jerky. "I do my best. So, what's your story?"

Rhode shrugged casually as if he didn't think much of it or he didn't think it was worth the breath to explain. "Moved here with my brother last week after he got assigned to the area."

"Is he like the military or something?"

"Something like that, it's more like private security."

"From Ireland? Isn't that where your accent is from?"

"It is Irish but I've been living in the States since I was ten or eleven; guess I haven't been properly Americanized out of it yet," he explained with a small smile. "What about you, darlin'? What's your story in this great big world?"

Now it was my turn not to think much of telling my story. "I used to live overseas with my mom, bouncing from country to country every few years."

"No accent on you, though," Rhode noted.

"Nah, we didn't start traveling until I was four or five, didn't leave the States until I was thirteen, and we never stayed in a country long enough for an accent to really stick. So, my accent, or lack thereof, is by default, I guess. I moved in with my sisters last year; my mom thought it would be better if I had some stability."

"So, where's your mom now?" he asked casually. "Still globetrotting?"

I took a visible pause before I spoke. "She died in a car accident shortly before I moved here."

"I'm sorry," he said in a low voice, those lovely toffee colored eyes watching me even closer after what I had just said.

I shook my head, trying to rid myself of the dark cloud that seemed to have formed around me. "No, it's fine. It's the first time I've ever said it out loud before."

"You said you moved here last year, right?" I nodded, sensing the direction he was headed with his questioning. "Why does it look like you're just as new as I am?"

I let out nervous laugh as tried to maintain my calm. "I was in the car with her."

Rhode's face fell and the air between us became tense and silent before he finally whispered, "Jesus, I'm sorry."

I shook my head. "We were just supposed to be going for a drive," I said softly as the memories started rushing back to me. "Some asshole ran us off a bridge and our car sank. I swam out and my mom said she was going to be right behind me." I looked at Rhode as I tapped my foot nervously. "She never surfaced. They never found her body either, said that it had probably been swept away with the current or something. I moved in with my sisters right after, but I was a mess. Wouldn't eat, couldn't sleep without nightmares, I didn't even talk for the first month after it happened. So, I was homeschooled for a year."

"Your sisters," Rhode said slowly, looking like he was trying to avoid any triggers, "are they okay with you being in public school now?"

I shrugged. "I think they think that it's good for me to get out and meet new people after being shut up in the house for so long."

"It must be working," he said with a small smile, "you're already making friends."

I couldn't help but let a smile form on my face. "Two loners uniting in weirdness, what better friendship is there?"

"Can I ask you something?" Rhode asked, his voice become low and serious again.

"You just did," I quipped, "but I'll give you a freebie."

A ghost of a smile appeared on his face but was gone by the time he spoke. "Did you try to kill yourself?" He motioned to my right arm, which I had now gotten into the habit of keeping tucked into my lap when I wasn't writing anything. "The scar on your wrist. It looks like . . ." He fell off, leaving a thick silence between us.

I gave him small smile and looked at him as I said evenly, "You seem like a smart guy Rhode. I wouldn't ruin a friendship over something that you can put together yourself."

I was more or less thankful that my last class of the day was gym, if what was going on even qualified as gym class. There was a clear divide in what was happening, all the students who played a sport were suited up and practicing while students who clearly had no interest in it sat on the grass and watched with mild interest. I was in the latter group and took the opportunity to start on my assignment for English while no one was paying me any attention.

"You," I heard someone call from across the field. I finished my sentence before looking up from my book, seeing a coach dressed in a black polo and khaki pants come across the feel toward me.

I looked up at him as he loomed over me as I sat uninitiated. "Yeah?"

He adjusted the black cap with the school mascot on it. "You Artemis Taylor?"

"I didn't do anything," I said, half unsure as I racked my brain through the events of the day.

The coach pointed over to where several students were lined up in three or four rows, shooting arrows at targets. "Get over there and fire some shots," the coach ordered.

I raised my eyebrow and held up my book. "I'm otherwise occupied, but thanks," I said, returning to the book.

"You get over there or you're going to spend the rest of the year running laps!" he barked.

I sighed and put down the book, feeling everyone stare at me as I made my way over to the archers. One of them handed me a bow and a quiver of arrows, and I could see the lines marked in ten foot intervals.

"Where do you want me to shoot from?" I asked the coach.

"Where can you shoot from?"

I didn't respond to the question, only looked at him, waiting for him to answer.

"Twenty feet," he said, clearly flustered regarding my attitude toward the situation.

I went to the line, rolling my neck as I had done this morning to loosen myself up. I took an arrow from the quiver and loosened my fingers quickly before I raised the bow and pulled the string back. I took three breathes and released on the third exhale.

Bullseye.

The coach wasn't fazed by it. "Baby steps, Taylor. Forty feet."

I walked back to the forty-foot line and raised my bow. Two deep breaths and I released on the second exhale.

Dead center.

"You made the team," he said after making shoot twice more. "Practice starts after school today."

"I don't want to be on the team."

"You're a nationally ranked archer, of course you want to be on the team." He looked at me as if I were speaking nonsense.

"My ranking has nothing to do with it." I was tired of everyone bringing it up, that was a long time ago and a different girl. "If I wanted to be on the team, I would have tried out. I don't so I didn't."

"So, you're just content to let your talent go to waste while you sit on the side line with those rejects?"

I eyed the coach as he gestured to the grass where I had been sitting with the others that had no interest in sports. I saw Rhode walk out to the grass and sit, our eyes meeting for a moment before he raised his brows.

No doubt confused as to why I was partaking in the jock mentality rather than sitting it out.

"Yeah," I said, a genuine smile forming on my face, "I guess I am."

"Just let her go, Coach." We both looked over to see a girl, a senior, standing behind us as she aimed her target from the fifty-foot line. She hit a bit left of the center but she looked at me with a smug smile as if she had done something worth writing the national news about. "She obviously doesn't have the talent to hack it with us."

I looked her over with her bottle-blond hair pulled back into a ponytail with her short shorts and tank top in the school colors. I might have had a class with her earlier today, but I had been on autopilot for the entirety of it so I wouldn't have remembered. I knew she took pleasure in making me feel like crap, but I wanted to take just as much pleasure in proving her wrong.

I shouldered the bow and quiver as I walked down to the very edge of the field, knowing that everyone out there watched me as I did so. I looked at the very last row of targets on the other side of the field as I took an arrow from the quiver and took aim.

Inhale.

On the exhale, I unleashed the arrows left in the quiver, watching as they flew across the field, hitting the long line of targets on the other side.

I walked back in silence, noting that all the arrows had all hit dead center on their targets. The coach and everyone else looked baffled and in awe as I walked back up to the coach and shoved the arrow and quiver at him.

"Like I said, I don't *want* a place on the team." I cast one last glance at the blonde bitch who thought I couldn't hack it, giving her a wink as I passed.

"Holy shit," someone said behind me as I walked off. "That's got to be over two-hundred feet."

"Nice shot, Legolas," Rhode said as he looked on with everyone else in wonder.

I didn't say anything, but I knew he saw the smile of satisfaction on my face as I walked back up the field to where the coach and other team members stood baffled. I cast a glance at my handy work—three of them were dead center, the other slightly left, but I chalked that up to the shift in wind.

The bell rang already for the end of school and everyone else sitting out had already taken off to get home. I swung my bag over my shoulder and Rhode put his arm around me as we walked back through the building. I could see people looking at us as we walked through the hall, looking like boyfriend and girlfriend even though I hadn't known this guy for more than a couple of hours. I took my time to revel the feeling, like I was normal again, like I had a life again.

"That was fucking awesome," Rhode said as we made our way outside. "Where'd you lean to shoot like that?"

I shrugged, honestly not sure where it had come from. "I've had lessons since I was thirteen, but my mom insisted that it's natural talent."

"You're telling me that you've always been able to shoot like that?"

"Practice makes perfect, but yeah, I've always been a really good shot. Ah, shit." I swore as we made it to the front of the school and my bus was nowhere to be seen. "I missed my bus."

"So did I," Rhode said as he looked around in vain.

"Well, I'm this way," I said.

"Up, just up that way," Rhode said at the same time and I noticed we were pointing in the same direction.

"Come on," I said with a smirk. "I could use some company."

"You mind?" Rhode asked after a few minutes, holding up a pack of cigarettes.

"Only if you share," I replied mildly. I wasn't new to this smoking scene, most of the people I hung out with in London could have doubled for chimneys. I wasn't a chain smoker but from time to time I'd partake just have some teenage rebellion to indulge in.

I watched as Rhode took two from the pack and placed them in his mouth. He lit them both in one strike, taking a puff off both of them before he took them out of his mouth and handed one to me. I took a puff with a small smile on my face, thinking about how the shared cigarette was like our first kiss.

"You're not scared of cancer?"

I took a long drag on the cigarette, letting the ash and smoke dance on my tongue before I let it out. "No. After a near death experience, you have a different perspective of what you're scared to die of."

Rhode stared at me and I smiled a little bit, putting a bit of bounce in my step as I widened my stride so that I could walk ahead of him and see the look on his face straight on. "Can I ask you something?"

I paused, finishing off my cigarette before I dropped it to the ground and crushed it beneath my heel. "Sure, as long it isn't what you've already asked me at lunch."

"No, it's not that." He paused for a moment and looked at me hard. "Are you a witch?"

I covered my mouth with my hand to avoid laughing right in his face. "Seriously? Like Charmed or Bewitched?" I had to stop as another laughing fit came on. "Sorry, I don't mean to laugh at you, but . . . seriously?"

Rhodes face softened a little at seeing my reaction to the question. "Sorry, I just saw this." He reached out and took my locket between his thumb and index finger, running over the pentagram on the top of it. "I saw this and I didn't know what to think."

"Oh," I said, some of the humor leaving my voice. "No, I think we're Jewish on my grandmother's side."

"Then why the pentagram?"

"This locket has been in our family for generations," I explained. "No one's really sure how far back it goes exactly, but my sister Eris says that it's traditionally given to the youngest daughter. No one knows why either."

"Holy shit," Rhode muttered.

"Yeah, the unofficial catchphrase of the Taylor family."

Rhode didn't say anything else for the rest of the walk home until we had reached my place. "This is me," Rhode said, pointing to the house next to mine.

"Ah, so you're the mysterious next door neighbors."

"Yeah, just moved in this morning."

"Artemis?" Rhea stood on the porch. My guess was that she had spotted Rhode and I walking together from down the street. She gave a polite smile and came over to where we were standing on the sidewalk, but I couldn't help but notice that her eyes had instantly locked onto Rhode. "Who's this?"

I sighed and played polite, making the introductions. "Ray, this is Rhode, he's our new neighbor. Rhode, this is my oldest sister Rhea."

"Please to meet you," Rhode said, offering his hand to her.

Rhea took it with a smile but I could see something dark behind her smile. "Likewise. I'm glad that Artemis is making friends so quickly."

"I should get going before my brother comes looking for me. I'll see you in class tomorrow?"

"Sure," I said, not being able to keep myself from smiling.

"Actually," Rhea interrupted before Rhode could make his escape. "Why don't you come inside for a little bit?"

I could see Rhode's hesitation, unsure of what Rhea's true intentions were behind the invitation. I didn't know myself and tried to ease Rhode's exit. "I don't want him to get in trouble with his brother, Ray."

"You live right next door," Rhea insisted, "I'm sure you'll be just fine. Come on, Eris is making brownies."

Rhode arched an eyebrow and looked at me with a sly grin. "Brownies?"

"Eris is a bit of a Suzie Homemaker," I offered.

"Then it's settled." Rhea sighed, turning on her heel and starting back inside.

Rhode and I followed a few feet behind her.

"I am so sorry," I whispered to Rhode. "My sister is really overprotective, but I didn't think she'd do this."

"No worries," Rhode said lightly, putting his arm around my shoulder and pulling me close to him as we walked. "I think I can handle your sisters. Besides, I love brownies."

Eris was pulling a tray of brownies out of the oven and cutting them into squares as Rhea came through the back door and into the kitchen, followed by Rhode and I. Eris's eyes lit up a bit at seeing Rhode and me standing together, his arm around my shoulder.

"Hello." Eris smiled warmly as she closed the over door. "Who's this?" she asked, gesturing to Rhode.

"This is Rhode," I said quietly. "Rhode, this is my other sister, Eris."

"I see your mother had a love of Greek mythology," Rhode commented.

Eris smiled politely but I could see the sadness behind it at the mention of Mom; even after all this time the wounds were still raw. "It was actually our grandmother," Eris explained. "Supposedly our grandfather was a

Greek man she had a fling with and supposedly that was our mother's father. She named her after the Goddess of the moon and I guess it just stuck through the next generation."

"I think the better the story behind a name, the more greatness that person is destined for," Rhode said with a gentle smile.

"I think I'm going to like you, neighbor boy," Eris said, the sadness in her vanishing. She handed me a plate of brownies she'd cut up and set on a plate. "Why don't we take these brownies to the table and you can tell me all about your day, little bird."

I could see Rhode slide an amused look in my direction as we all sat down around the kitchen table. "Little bird?" he mouthed at me.

I made a silly face at him and took a bite from my brownie and said, "They offered me a spot on the archery team."

"What?" Rhea's outraged voice filled the room and bounced off the walls before plunging everyone into a long moment of complete silence.

"I didn't know you tried out," Eris said calmly.

"I didn't, the coach heard about me and gave me the option of shooting arrows or running laps. I chose the former."

"Can't say I'm surprised," Eris muttered, knowing my aversion to physical activity unless absolutely necessary.

"Needless to say, he was impressed and gave me a spot on the team which I politely declined."

"Jesus, hasn't that school heard of parental permission?" Rhea asked.

"Apparently not," I answered.

"She was amazing to watch," Rhode said softly. "She shot an arrow clear across the football field and hit dead center. Your sister has some serious talent."

"That she does," Rhea affirmed, her eyes shifting to Rhode. "So, tell us about yourself Rhode. You're new to New Orleans, right?"

"Yeah, got here about a week ago, but we finally bought a house in our price range. That's why we're moving in just now."

"Where did you live before then?" Rhea asked.

"Ireland originally, but we've been bouncing around from place to place for my brother's job."

"What would that be in?" Rhea probed, but her polite tone had failed her and now even Rhode could see through her guise.

"Private security," he answered politely.

"Private security?" Rhea prodded, her interest peeked. "What does that entail?"

Rhode just shrugged. "He doesn't talk about it a lot, it's mostly escorting rich socialites to parties and making sure that they get back home safe. The money's pretty good, but it does make for some late hours."

"That must be lonely for you," Eris said softly.

"Not so much after a while," Rhode remarked with a soft smile. "I like the quiet, I can get a lot of reading done."

"So, how did you meet Artemis exactly?" Rhea asked, pretending as if she had forgotten if the topic had even been mentioned.

"Rhode and I have history together and we have gym the same period, so we're on the field together," I said, casting a long side eye at Rhea.

A knock at the front door cut through the small silence that had filled the room. Eris got up and went to answer the door. "Can I help you?"

Over her shoulder I could see a tall man standing just outside the door with an angry scowl on his face. He didn't say anything, he simply pointed at Rhode and signaled him to follow.

"Shit," Rhode breathed, "busted."

It took me a moment before I noticed the similar features Rhode shared with the man—the same shade of brown hair and brown eyes, though Rhode's eyes were considerably lighter. The two of them even shared the same tall, slim, and muscular build.

"That's your brother," I realized.

"Yeah, and he's not happy, but then again he never really is."

"I hope I didn't get you in trouble," Rhea said, apologetic.

"It's okay," Rhode said, shirking off the apology. "He would have found a reason to chew me out today anyway."

"I'll see you in class tomorrow?" I was unsure if he even wanted to have anything to do with me after what happened today.

"Wouldn't miss it." He smiled, giving me quick wink before he got up and left out the front door. Rhea followed Rhode to the door and closed it behind him, locking it as soon as it was shut.

"You want to tell me what all that was about?"

I looked over at Rhea, but she was standing by the window watching

Rhode's house like a hawk. "I want you to stir clear of the new neighbors until we can decide what's what."

"What are you talking about?" My outrage snapped me out of the numb state I had been in. "Rhode is the only friend I have, why would I avoid him?"

"I just want to get a vibe for them before everyone gets chummy."

Eris, being the buffer she's always been, stepped in on my behalf. "Ray, we can't isolate ourselves from everyone because you think they're coming after Artemis?"

The last part had put me off guard. "What are you talking about? Who's after me?"

Rhea looked straight at Eris, both of them ignoring my question. "I wouldn't be able to forgive myself if something happened to her," she said slowly in a low tone.

"We can trust Rhode and his brother," I interjected. "I can feel it in my bones."

Rhea took a moment, mulling it over before answering. "You're really sure we can trust them?"

"If we can't, then I'll take care of it myself," I said darkly. It didn't matter how much I liked to party and how much I missed being a social butterfly, if someone posed a threat to my sisters then I would put them in the ground.

Rhea sighed and after a moment said, "Fine. You can hang out with Rhode, but be careful, we still don't know what's going on yet."

Chapter 3

Mom always told me that if I never went to college I would make an amazing grifter, she always said that lying was a trade I excelled in. She wasn't wrong in that. After dinner, I was in my room, reading *Wuthering Heights* with the television on in the background to help engage my ADD mentality. The story was a good one, but it was depressing as fuck—those Bronte sisters really knew how to take love and make it dark.

"Artemis," Eris's voice came softly at the door that was left open a crack. She opened it all the way and leaned in the threshold looking at me. "How are you doing?"

"I'm fine, just getting this reading done for school tomorrow."

"I know everything that's going on right now is overwhelming—I've been there before—but things haven't changed as much as you think they have."

"Really?" I had quite a few points to counter.

"Yeah, really. Rhea and I and are still your sisters and we both still love you. You're still you, Artemis, now you're just now a little more."

I didn't say anything, unsure how I would even respond to that.

"You know that Ray is hard on you because she cares about you, right?"

"I know."

"Good. I'm headed to bed. Give a shout if you need anything." Eris fell off and we both sat in the awkwardness of the moment as we remembered my night terrors that caused me to wake in the middle of the night screaming so loud the neighbors would call the cops.

"Nightmare humor," I said dryly. "Hilarious. Good night." I gave her a little smile so she knew I was fine, or at least so she could have the illusion of it for a few hours.

"Good night, little bird." She blew me a kiss before she left, closing the door behind her.

I kept reading for a little while longer when a tapping sound at my window startled me. I looked up from the book and saw Rhode outside my bedroom window. I stared at him in shock for a moment before I finally spoke. "What are you doing?" I asked in a hushed whispered.

"Come on and let me in."

"Yeah, because letting a guy I just met today into my room in the middle of the night is an amazing idea." I rolled my eyes.

"I'm not trying to get into your pants if that's what you're worried about."

I opened the window and leaned against the sill, looking at Rhode. "What if I'm worried about you murdering me?"

"I'm pretty sure your sister interrogating me over brownies and milk was designed to eliminate that possibility."

"Sorry about that," I said, backing up a bit and allowing him into my room. He had barely stood up fully when I pulled out the knife I had hidden in the back pocket of my jeans. I held the tip underneath Rhode's chin and could feel his body stiffen, trying not to move an inch. "Just so you know, I don't need my sisters to protect me. I can take care of myself."

"I have no doubt of that, darlin'," he said, his eyes trained on me until I put the knife away. "I just thought you were lonely and wanted to talk."

I backed up until I felt my legs hit the edge of the bed. Eyeing my new neighbor warily, I sat down on the edge of the bed. "What's your brother going to say if he catches you over here with me?"

"Let me worry about him," Rhode responded, but I couldn't help noticing he didn't answer my question. "What happens if your sisters find me in here with you?"

"Then I'm back to not having any friends," I answered darkly. I looked up at Rhode as he watched me carefully. "So, what do you want to talk about?"

"Anything you want, I'm not exactly picky," Rhode said, walking the space between us slowly, sitting next to me on the edge of the bed. "Your hopes and dreams, maybe?"

"What hopes and dreams?" I asked, feeling the bitterness in my tone.

"I'm broken, Rhode. I've been traumatized and I'm always going to be treated like that. The best I can hope for is to just be normal again."

"You must have wanted to be something before all of this happened. What did you want to do with your life before the accident?"

I fell back onto the bed, staring at the ceiling as I tried to think of an answer. "I don't really know. I was young and we traveled a lot, so my focus in life was to just party and have fun. I was pretty aimless. Maybe I still am."

Rhode looked down at me and I could see something on his face that I couldn't place. "Just give it some time, Artemis," he said softly. "I think you're destined for greatness."

"Yeah?" I asked, surprised by his optimism. "Well I think you're full of shit."

Rhode gave a dark chuckle and leaned back on the bed next to me. "Maybe I am, darlin'," he conceded softly. "Maybe I am."

I rolled over onto my side, facing Rhode across the space between us on the bed. He reached out slowly and placed his hand on the back of my neck, his thumb brushing over the spot behind my ear where I had my most recent tattoo.

"I saw it behind your ear when we were talking earlier, but I didn't get a chance to ask you about it." Rhode asked softly, "What is it?"

"A semicolon," I answered.

"I see that. What does it mean?"

"Maybe one day I'll tell you," I said slowly, seeing how intently he watched me even in the dim light of the room.

"Got any more tattoos?"

"Hmm, wouldn't you like to know?"

Rhode and I talked for the rest of the night, holding conversations about things that seemed so insignificant. He made me laugh, genuinely laugh for the first time in I didn't know how long, the two of us just talking and laughing and enjoying each other's company until we both fell asleep.

I would have said that it was one of the best nights I had in a long time, in fact, maybe it still was, but in my experience every good always has a bad. I barely remembered falling asleep and I don't remember what the nightmare was even about. All I remembered was sitting up as I screamed myself awake, calling out for my mother who could no longer save me.

It took a moment to collect myself, realizing that I was in my room in New Orleans with my sisters when toffee brown eyes stared at me through the dark, the light of the moon the only illumination.

"Are you okay?" Rhode's voice came through the dark so softly, and for a moment I thought he was part of my dream.

"Yeah," I crocked out. "Bad dreams."

"That didn't seem like a bad dream to me," Rhode said, his voice concerned. He moved closer to me on the bed, but I got up from the bed, my mind spinning for a moment.

"You got to hide," I said in a rushed whispered.

"What?" he asked, confused by my order.

"Artemis?" Eris's voice came from the other side of the door. It wasn't often that either of my sisters had checked on me after I had a nightmare, this must have been a really bad one to make Eris come check on me.

I looked at Rhode with wide eyes and pointed at the closet. "Hide," I mouthed as I went to the door and opened it.

"You okay, little bird?" Eris asked as she came inside, the light from the hall illuminating her blonde hair that tousled from restless sleep. "I heard you screaming."

I looked over nervously at the closet but breathed a sigh of relief at seeing that Rhode had managed to hide himself in the closet in time. "I'm fine, Eris, I must've fallen asleep reading and had a bad dream."

"You sure you're okay?" She leveled her gaze at me.

"I'm fine," I assured her. "I'm just going to get changed and shoot a few arrows before school."

"Okay, I'll be in my room if you need me."

"Thanks, Eris." I gave her a small smile before she left the room again.

Once I was sure Eris was out of earshot, I went to the closet and opened it, seeing Rhode standing amongst my clothes. "Coast clear?" he asked.

"I think you should get home," I offered, "thanks for the company."

Rhode made his way to the window and paused for a moment. "What are you going to do now? I don't think I could go back to sleep, and I didn't even have the nightmare."

"I was going to do some target practice, help calm myself down."

"Can I watch?"

"Free country, but you got to take the window down."

Rhode gave me a little smirk before he tucked out the window and disappeared the way he had come.

Once I changed and made my way down to the backyard with my bow and arrow, Rhode was lying on the lawn, staring up at the dark sky now conceding to the rising sun and the light it brought.

I sat down on the grass next to him and he turned to look at me as I stretched out the way I did every morning. "You do this every morning?" He watched me carefully.

"Only when I can't sleep," I answered. "So, yeah, I do this every morning."

"Your nightmares are that bad?" He proceeded with his line of questioning carefully, but we both knew where it was headed.

"They used to be a lot worse. Right after the accident I wouldn't sleep more than a couple hours at a time because the night terrors were so bad." I lifted my left arm to show him the tattoo of a dream catcher that I had underneath my upper arm. "I got this about four or five months after everything happened, just hoping that it would all stop."

"Did it?"

I gave him a look that asked *What do you think?* but I humored him nonetheless. "They've gotten better and, at this point, I guess it's all I can ask for."

"What are they about? If you don't mind my asking."

"I don't remember some of them," I admitted. "Most of the time it's me remembering the accident." I cleared my throat and stood up off the grass. "Honestly, I try not to think about it."

Rhode brushed himself off and stood up as well. "You think you could teach me how to shoot?" He gestured to my bow.

I looked at him for a long moment. "Sure, show me what you got, cowboy." I stepped back and allowed Rhode to pick up the bow and an arrow, laughing a bit to myself as he tried and failed the first couple of times to pull the string back properly. On the third attempt, he had actually pulled it back and took aim, but sadly the arrow only made it a couple of feet before it made contact with the lawn.

I watched as he attempted again, walking around behind him and placing both my hands on either of his shoulders. "Relax," I said softly, and I could feel his muscles relax beneath my hands. "It's not just about strength. It's about control and focus. Focus on your target and let go."

Rhode inhaled a long breath before he unleashed the arrow, making contact with the target on the farthest outer circle.

"Not bad," I said, actually impressed, and I didn't impress easily.

"Yeah, well, I think I'll leave the badass arrow wielding to you." Rhode handed my bow back to me.

"Rhode!" a deep voice barked from across the yard.

Rhode and I turned to see his brother standing at the fence line, looking at the both of us with a livid expression.

"Busted again," Rhode said, "but it was totally worth it this time."

I couldn't stop the grin from coming to my lips. "I'll see you in class?"

"Rabid, wild dogs couldn't keep me away, darlin'." He smiled. "Thanks for the company." He gave me a wink before turning around and jogging toward the fence and hopping over. I watched as Rhode's brother started yelling at him, probably for being out all night, but I didn't miss Rhode's cocky grin failing to falter all the way into the house.

After talking all night, there was one thing I knew for sure about Rhode, that boy was definitely something else.

Chapter 4

The second day of school didn't really differ from the first in my opinion. Then again, I didn't exactly have a high opinion of high school. I spent first period with my nose stuck in a copy of *The Bell Jar* as the teacher droned on about calculus. I knew Rhea would rip me a new one if she saw me like this at school, but if I failed senior year then at least I had leverage for homeschooling.

Second period was French and I was in the process of spending my time reading when I heard someone take the seat next to me. "Sylvia Plath, huh?" Caleb's voice came from next to me. "That's an interesting choice."

"Yeah, well, I said that I might surprise you." I turned to see Caleb smiling at me with those movie star white teeth, the best money could buy. "I didn't know you had French this period, I didn't see you yesterday."

"I just got my transfer to this class approved. My parents wanted me to take Spanish, but seeing as I never plan on leaving New Orleans, I thought French would be more in my favor. Clearly, it's already paying off."

Jesus, he was a flirt. "Yeah, well don't expect to copy off me during test, foreign languages aren't exactly my forte."

"Word around the rumor mill is that you been to a bunch of different countries over the years."

"Yes," I affirmed, "and I've learned to swear and ask for a beer in every single one of those languages. Conversational phrases never really stuck around."

Caleb laughed at that, not a chuckle but a full-toothed, over the top laugh that stopped the entire class. I pretended I had nothing to do with any of this until he had finished his little episode and class resumed.

"You should sit with me at lunch, meet my friends," Caleb offered.

"No thanks, Sylvia and I have a lunch date at the loner table."

"Are you sure that's what you want to do?" he asked carefully. "Once you get branded a loner, that's usually where you stay."

"I'll take my chances, but thanks." I turned my attention back to my book.

"That new kid you were hanging out with yesterday is gonna drag you down," Caleb said, his voice low and serious. "You have a chance to make friends and be happy here, don't let him blow that for you."

I set my book down and looked at Caleb. "You don't know anything about me or my life to make those kinds of statements."

"I'm just trying to be your friend here."

"If you want to be my friend," I snapped. "You'll think next time before you decide to speak to me."

I pulled my headphones out of my pocket and put them in, drowning out the sounds of both my French teacher and the asshole jock sitting next to me. This was going to be a long school year.

Caleb had basically shattered my mood and, when I made it to history class for third period, Rhode could tell before I even sat down.

"What's wrong?"

"Just in a bad mood right now, I'll be fine in a little bit." I turned to look at him, trying to turn the conversation toward him. "Did everything go okay with your brother this morning?"

Rhode just shrugged. "Same old, same old. He told me to get myself together or he'd send me to military school, but I know he won't do it. I think he's trying to scare me straight."

"What happens when you call his bluff?"

"I'll never call his bluff. I may be reckless, but I'm not stupid."

I shook my head at the comment, pinching the bridge of my nose as the gesture set off pain behind my eyes.

"You okay?"

"Yeah. I've just been fighting a headache since this morning."

Rhode reached out and touched my face gently, letting his thumb run down the back of my ear. I sighed as he started to rub small circles against the pressure point and the pain started to alleviate. "Better?"

I nodded. "Much."

"You're really cold." Rhode shrugged out of his jacket and offered it to me in on smooth motion.

"I'm fine. I don't need your jacket."

"Take it," he insisted. "Chivalry and all that jazz."

I rolled my eyes at him, taking the jacket and putting it on. It was three sizes too big and swallowed me up, but as I snuggled into the warmth of his smell, I realized just how chilled my body had been.

The bell rang and Mr. Black went straight to work, talking away at warp speed as everyone tried their hardest to keep up with what was being said. I doodled in my notebook, faking my attention to the Thirteen Colonies and the Revolutionary War, knowing Rhode would give me the notes to copy later.

My pen froze as I heard the sound of heavy footfalls walk up the aisle up the middle aisle of the room, making its way toward the front. I watched as a pair of black combat boots made their way past where I sat, the chill I had been feeling intensifying as they did so.

I looked up, pretending I was checking what was written on the board, but something else caught my eye. My finger became numb and the pen fell from my hand as I saw a tall dark figure standing at the board next to the teacher. The figure was wearing all-black clothing and a long black coat that went to the floor with the boots that I had seen walk past me. I couldn't see the figure's face as it was hidden behind a faceless white mask that only had holes for the eyes.

I took in a shaking breath, seeing the figure look at me. "Ahh, you *can* see me," the figure said with a smile in their voice.

Any answer that was on my tongue had been snatched away by the Arctic chill this figure brought with them. I shivered in my seat, trying desperately to keep my teeth from chattering as I tried to wake up from this nightmare I'd found myself in.

"Are you okay?" Rhode asked, noticing me sitting there, staring unblinking at this figure no one else seemed to be able to see. He reached out and touched my hand. "Artemis? What's wrong?"

I didn't answer him, my voice too shaken to talk, my body too frozen to run. The figure started walking toward me, keeping their eyes locked firmly on mine. Fear made my heart feel as if it were about to jump out of my chest.

"Tell me," the masked figure continued. "Why can you see me?"

Adrenaline coursed through my veins and I shot to my feet, knocking over my stool as I struggled on wobbling legs to the front of the classroom.

"Miss Taylor?" Mr. Black stopped his lightning lecture and turned his attention toward me. "Is everything alright?"

"Nurse," I stammered out, unsure if my voice was even loud enough for him to hear me.

I didn't know what the fuck was going on, but I couldn't breathe and my best guess was a panic attack triggered by God knows whatever that thing was. I leaned against the teacher's desk, because at the moment it was the only thing keeping my head from meeting the floor.

"Artemis?" I managed to turn and see Rhode standing up in his seat as he watched me with worried eyes. "Talk to me, what's going on?"

I was struggling to find the words in my throat, but I could see the dark figure standing behind Rhode, who was oblivious to the fact that he was there.

"Tell me, girl. What else do you see?"

The chill that I felt from the figure swept through me again at the question and I shook even harder. I locked eyes with Rhode as he rushed toward me as I felt myself start to drop like a stone, but I was gone before I even hit the floor.

I woke with a start, but there was no strength left in me to even lift my head and it fell back onto the surface of wherever I was laying. I reached up to touch my temple as a raging headache pounded through me like a lightning strike.

"Hey there," a soft voice came from over me. "You're okay now."

My eyes fluttered open and saw that I was lying on a small cot in the nurse's office. Rhode sat in a chair beside the cot, watching me very closely. "Rhode?" I managed to get out, my voice barely a whisper.

"Welcome back. How do you feel?"

"Freezing," I answered, curling up as best I could underneath the thin blanket that had been laid over me, but it did nothing to ease the chill I felt from that figure. "My head hurts, too."

Rhode reached out and brushed his fingertips against my temple. I closed my eyes for a moment, the touch offering a moment of relief before another shiver racked my body.

Rhode's brow furrowed with worry. "What happened back there?"

"I don't remember," I lied, knowing that telling Rhode about the dark figure would only make me seem crazy. I couldn't take that chance with the only friend I had. "I think I'm sick with the flu or something."

"The nurse called your sisters to come and get you. They should be here any minute," he said as if I needed the reassurance of that fact. "Just get some rest, okay?"

I nodded weakly, closing my eyes and drifting away almost immediately into darkness.

"WAKE UP, ARTEMIS," a voice called through the darkness that I had nestled myself into.

"Let me sleep," I grumbled, curling up tighter under the blanket.

"You've been asleep all day, little bird," the voice countered. "You need to wake up and eat something."

"Not hungry," I groaned.

"Come on," the voice coaxed, "come back to the real world."

Slowly and with every fiber or strength in my being, I listened and opened my eyes, seeing Eris kneeling over me. She smiled when our eyes met, stroking the hair back from my face. I took a moment to collect myself and sat up, noticing I was no longer in the nurse's office at school, I was on the couch in the living room at home. I looked around in a bit of shock, seeing the light that filtered through the windows was low and golden, the sun almost gone from the sky.

"What happened?" I touched my head as the traces of my headache still lingered.

"I was hoping that was something that you could tell me," Eris said. There was something behind her eyes that I couldn't place, as if she were hiding something from me. "Come on, let's get something in your stomach."

I knew better than to argue with her, so I followed her into the kitchen, wrapping my blanket around me as I sat at the table. Eris took no time in placing a bowl of soup in front of me. I ate half the bowl before pushing it away, my stomach doing so many flip flops I was afraid I wasn't going to be able to keep it down.

"Do you want to tell me what happened?" Eris asked slowly. She had been watching me the entire time I ate, as if I would fall over at any moment.

"Just bits and pieces. I was in class and I saw something," I started, stopping for a moment to think about what Eris would say if I told her about the shadowy figure. "I thought I saw something and I guess it just triggered a panic attack. I fainted and woke up in the nurse's office. That's all I remember."

"What did you see?" she asked, her eyes steady with mine as she tried to read my body language.

"I saw this figure. I couldn't tell if was a man or a woman, but they had this white mask on their face."

"A white mask?"

I nodded. "Yeah, all I could see was the eyes, and it was dressed head-to-toe in black. It was just so weird."

"Did anyone else see this figure?"

I shook my head, slowly questioning my sanity as I told this story and heard it out loud. "No, that's why I thought it was just a figment of my imagination, but it couldn't have been. The chill I felt from that thing cut through me like ice, and I know I didn't imagine that." I paused for a moment as I tried to piece together everything that had happened since history class, but I just kept coming up short. "How did I get home?"

"Only my baby sister could have slept through all of that." A small smile came to her face. "We couldn't wake you in the nurse's office, so Rhode offered to carry you to the car. Getting you in the house from the car was a feat that I owe to P90X. You were out like a light. Have any good dreams?"

I shook my head. "I didn't dream at all. It was a little weird, actually."

"Rhea will be getting back from work any minute. Why don't you go take a shower and rest a little more? I'll come check on you later." Eris leaned in and kissed my forehead before she took the bowl and started busying herself again. I watched her for a little while, our eyes catching each other every so often, but I could tell she and Rhea were hiding something.

That figure I saw today was real, and Eris knew that. There was something my sisters weren't telling me, and I knew it had to do with what I saw today. I just had to figure out what.

Chapter 5

By the time I finished taking my shower and changing, Rhea was already home from work; she fused over me for half an hour before Eris pulled her off and allowed me some alone time. I sat on my bed, wrapped in my blanket, staring outside my bedroom window and into Rhode's window, hoping to catch a glance of him, but the window was dark and I was sure I wouldn't see him again tonight.

I settled into bed and closed my eyes, laying there in the dark as I listened to the sounds of Eris and Rhea fretting over me from downstairs. When I heard a sound coming from my window, I didn't move, I just lay still as it opened and familiar footprints made their way across the room.

I felt better for some reason when I felt the mattress sink further and strong arms wrap around me. "You really worried me today." Rhode's voice came softly as he spoke into my hair. "When you fainted, all I could think was to catch you and to make sure you were alright."

"You carried me all the way to the nurse's office?"

"It just sort of happened," he explained, as he started to lace his fingers through mine. "Like a reflex."

"Well, thank you," I said. "For being my knight in shining armor."

"You're welcome. Are you feeling better?"

"I am," I answered rather truthfully. I really did feel better now that Rhode was with me, but I didn't really know why; maybe we just click on some level. Being around him felt natural and made me at ease.

"Are you feeling well enough to go on a little field trip?"

"A field trip where?"

"I want to take you to the French Quarter, show you the real New Orleans."

I rolled over onto my other side so I could look at Rhode face to face—he had that cocky smirk on his face as if it were permanently attached. "You've been here less time than I have, how do you know what the real New Orleans is?"

"Ah," he said, his grin getting wider as if I had fallen into a trap he'd set for me. "I said that we had just moved here, I never said I hadn't been here before."

"You've been to New Orleans before?"

"This is the first place we lived after leaving Dublin. We stayed a couple of years and bounced around between states, but we've come back to this beautiful city many times. Every time we come back, I go to the Quarter to celebrate my return to my surrogate home. Now I have someone to celebrate with."

"My sisters will notice if I'm gone, they'll be checking on me, especially after today."

"Come on," he coaxed. "We'll drive over and have a beignet or two, maybe hear some music, and we'll be back before your sisters even know you're gone."

"What about your brother? Isn't he going to be mad when he finds out you took his car to the French Quarter in the middle of the night?"

Rhode got up off the bed and back toward the window slowly. "Maybe I'm stupid enough to call his bluff about military school tonight."

I sat up, still on the fence on whether to go gallivanting around with a guy I've known a grand total of two days. "I thought you said you weren't stupid enough to call his bluff?"

He shrugged a shoulder, trying to make light of this decision and its possible consequences. "Maybe it's worth it to call his bluff just to spend the night with you," he said honestly. "Are you in or out?"

I looked at him through the dim light of the room, thinking about this boy who lived next door, the one that intrigued me and made me laugh. The first person who hadn't made me feel like a freak or a by-product of tragedy.

"I'm in."

I knew this boy was definitely something else, and I didn't know what that was yet, but I was drawn to him like a magnet, and for good or bad, I was sneaking out with him tonight. I was going to have myself an adventure.

After Rhode and I managed to sneak out the window, hop the fence to his house and steal his brother's car without getting caught, we drove down to the French Quarter. Rhode parked and we walked the streets as I took in the lights and the music and the nightlife as if it threatened to devour me.

Rhode took me to a little cafe just off Bourbon Street; it was a small place, but it was cute and there seemed to be a stream of customers coming in and out, ordering food. We were seated in a table in the corner. I looked around, taking in everything I could lay my eyes on, but it was only when I saw the way Rhode stared at me that I realized I looked like a patient that had just been released from an insane asylum.

"Sorry," I apologized, suddenly very self-conscious that his eyes were on me.

"No worries, darlin.'" he smiled. "How long has it been since you've left the house and been in the real world?"

"A year," I confessed. "I was in a hospital in London after the accident for a couple of days. Rhea and Eris came to get me and took me home and that was the last time I was out."

"Really?" Rhode asked, almost surprised that I really hadn't gone out for that stretch of time.

"My sisters tried. God help them, they tried," I explained. "They would try to get me to go on walks or even just to the store, but I was just so far gone at that point, I don't even think I really heard them."

"I take it their methods fell short," he speculated.

"They managed to get me out to the cemetery for my mother's funeral," I said, the words falling out numbly. "I don't even remember most of it, but something happened and I just lost it. I started bawling my eyes out and screaming. Freaked everyone out. I was inconsolable for days and I think that was when I just made a choice to stay locked away from the world."

"Well, I'm glad you decided to come out of hiding, darlin'. Don't think I would have the pleasure of meeting you if you didn't."

A small trace of a smile came to my lips as the waiter came over to us. She was a young girl, about mid-twenties, with caramel-colored skin and dark curly hair pulled back into a ponytail. "What can I get you folks tonight?" she asked, flashing a dazzlingly white smile at us.

"Uh," I started, faltering immediately and feeling super embarrassed. "I don't know what to order."

I think Rhode could feel my cheeks flush. "Two beignets, please." He smiled, stepping in for me.

"Coming up," she said, her Creole accent more prevalent now, before she turned away and flounced back to the counter.

"Sorry," I muttered, staring down at my hands intently. "Just remembered that I've never been here before. Not really, anyway."

"You never came to visit your sisters here?" Rhode asked.

"No, once Mom left for Europe, we never came back. The only time I ever saw Eris or Ray is if they came to whatever country we were in to visit."

"So, what's your favorite food, then?"

I looked up at him and could tell he was trying to make me feel better and that he didn't want me to feel embarrassed in front of him. "I really love Thai," I admitted. "There was this place in London that had this really amazing curry and I just kind of fell in love with it. We never made it to Asia, so I didn't get a chance to find it firsthand. I love Mexican too, never got a chance to go there either. What about you?"

"I didn't have a favorite type of food until I first came here," he answered with a small smile, as if he were recalling and savoring that memory. "I fell in love with French and Creole cooking, and no matter where I go, it never tastes the same as home."

Our waitress came back over, setting down a plate in front of each of us before flouncing off again. I did have to give it to Rhode, he never looked at her ass once. I picked up the fried treat, shaking some of the powdered sugar off in the process. "What are these things supposed to be, anyways?"

"Beignet? Think of them like a big fried donut, covered in sugar."

He sat there patiently, waiting for me to take the first bite. I took a bite and smiled in sheer delight as the doughy, sweet goodness filled my mouth. "Oh my God," I said around a mouthful. "This is possibly one of the best things I've ever tasted in my life."

"Glad you like it." Rhode chuckled, finally digging into his own food. "Didn't really think you would since I never see you eat anything."

I paused and set down my beignet. "I eat all the time."

"I see you snack on little things, but I've never really seen you eat a full meal before." He paused immediately after he had said it. "If you have an eating disorder . . ." He fell off again.

"I don't have an eating disorder," I told him evenly. "I told you how was in the hospital for a couple of days after the accident, right?"

Rhode nodded. "Yeah."

"I didn't eat anything the entire time I was there, I was in too much shock or something, I guess. They didn't even want to release me because they were concerned about my welfare, but Ray and Eris were desperate to get me back here. When my sisters got me home, they tried to get me to eat, but I just wasn't there," I said, touching my head to indicate that I was mentally gone.

Rhode didn't say anything, looking at me intently as I told my story.

"I was just having my own pity party that I didn't bother to take care of myself. If my sisters weren't constantly taking care of me and watching me, I don't even know what have would happened. It took months for me to even try and get my shit together and, as I started to recover, things started to fall back into place, but sometimes it's just a little too easy to fall back into old patterns. That's why I always have snacks and Eris is always baking cookies or brownies; I think she's more terrified than anybody that I'll relapse."

"Wow."

"Yeah, I've never told anyone that before."

I looked at Rhode as if the pieces were starting to fit together between us. I had trusted this guy enough to take me out in the middle of the night, and now I had trusted him with a story that I hadn't told anyone, ever. There was one thing that tonight taught me, I could trust Rhode O'Brian, without falter or a doubt.

After the cafe, Rhode took me to a bar a few blocks over to hear some jazz music. We sat at the bar, just listening, when the bartender came up and asked what we wanted to drink. I think my answer of straight whiskey both shocked and surprised Rhode. It was good to know that I still have a few surprises left in me.

I sat there on my bar stool, leaning against the counter as I drank my whisky, thinking about all the nights of youth that felt so far away now. "I used to go to places like these," I reminisced, my drink going to my head, I was sure.

"Where?" Rhode asked softly.

"Wherever I was with whatever friends that I had at the stretch of time," I answered.

"What kind of music did you listen to?"

"Didn't matter," I said, a bit of sadness creeping into my voice. "Pop, hip-hop, punk, metal, electronic. I've heard them all a million times before. Never jazz, though." I fell off taking a sip of my drink, letting the alcohol burn all the way down as it took some of the pain away.

"So, you used to sneak out of the house and go to bars to get drunk and listen to music?"

I tipped my glass back slowly, draining the rest of its contents with a sinful smile. I leaned my head back and looked at Rhode, who had been keeping a very close eye on me all night. "I used to dance," I said slowly, my words slurring a little. "I used to love to dance."

A slow song started to play and I watched as Rhode reached out his hand and took mine, standing up off his bar stool. "Let's dance then," he said, pulling me out of my seat.

I didn't protest or ask why, just followed him as he led me out into an open area other couples had started dancing in. Rhode pulled me close and I rested my head on his shoulder as we swayed back and forth to the music. We didn't talk, choosing instead to enjoy that song, that moment together where we were just two teenagers with not a care in the world . . . before that illusion was shattered.

The song came to an end and, with it, the passing moment the two of us shared together. I checked the time on my watch, noticing that we had been gone about an hour and a half. "Let's get going," I prompted. "We still have time to get back home before anyone knows that we're gone."

"Not just yet," Rhode said slowly. "There's one more place I want you to see."

"A FORTUNE TELLER?" I stared up at the bright neon sign that hung over the shop that Rhode had brought me to.

"She reads tarot cards," Rhode clarified.

"A fortune teller," I reiterated.

"Not a fortune teller," Rhode insisted.

"I don't believe in this kind of stuff, Rhode. They're just grifters and swindlers, she can't tell me anything that isn't just broad speculation, or even just guessing."

"Come on, you're not open to a just a little bit of magic, even in New Orleans?"

"I'm a skeptic, sue me."

"Ten minutes," he coaxed. "We'll be in and out and you'll be back home before your sisters even know you're gone."

I stared at him for a long moment, before he put on a sad puppy dog look that I couldn't help but laugh at. "Fine," I caved, "ten minutes, and if this chick is a fake you owe me twenty bucks."

"You're on, darlin'." He grinned, taking my hand and leading me inside.

The inside of the shop was covered in brightly colored scarves and curtains that made me feel like I was inside the bottle from *I Dream of Jeannie.* There was a large table in the center of the room where I guessed business was handled. The place smelled like sage and jasmine and, for some reason, I got chills.

A beaded curtain rattled and a woman in her late thirties came out, wearing a loose multicolored dress, and her hair was wrapped up in teal-colored scarf. "Madame Josephine," she announced herself. "At your service."

She gave a little bow before walking over to the table, beckoning us to do this same. We sat down, but there was something in my gut that told me I didn't want to hear anything this woman wanted to say to me, true or not.

"What can I do for you this evening?" Madame Josephine put on a thick fake French accent, as if she thought we were just some tourists.

"My friend wants to have her cards read," Rhode explained, putting his arm around me as if he could feel my anxiety.

Madame Josephine nodded, pulling out a pair of what looked like playing cards, but they were thicker. She placed them on the table and began to shuffle them as she looked at me dubiously. "You are not a believer of the arts?"

"No, I'm not a fan of getting conned," I answered.

"You should respect the spirits and what they have to say, *Cherie.* You'll find that you'll need them in time."

"Can you just read my cards so I can get out of her please?" My heart suddenly felt like it was beating a million beats per minute. "I'm kind of breaking curfew here."

Madame Josephine nodded, flipping over several cards and staring at them for a few long moments. "You have strong women that lead you in life," she started. "Your mother and your sisters, but I see that your mother is no longer with you, she is on her own journey."

"No, she's not," I corrected. "She's dead."

Madame Josephine gave me a look but didn't respond. "I do see love in your life. A love so great that it will connect you at the very core, but this love will not be easy. You must fight to keep it or your enemies will take it away from you."

"What enemies?" I asked breathlessly, unable to keep the question from tumbling out of my mouth.

"You have power that you have yet to realize," Madame Josephine continued. "The knowledge of this power will rip the world as you know it apart, but it will make you stronger. Your strength and the power that you wield will change everything you and all others of your kind will know."

"What power?" I shook my head as all her words started to swim around my head, confusing me. "My kind? What are you talking about?"

She didn't answer me, she only looked back down at the cards. "I see that you are surrounded by warriors," she continued. "Some of them are here to protect you, but there are others that will try to destroy you. There is an older man, a man from your past, who will try to destroy you. He will wield a weapon in the form of a young warrior, another man from your past, but this one is torn. This young man can be your destruction or your salvation."

I was out of my seat and making a direct escape from the shop before I had even realized what I was doing. I rushed out to meet the muggy night air, breathing in as much air as my lungs could take, but it still didn't seem to be enough.

"Artemis!" Rhode came rushing out of the shop after me. "What's going on?"

I wiped away a tear that had slipped down my cheek. I hadn't even realized that I had been crying. "Nothing," I said, but my voice was frightened and I couldn't make that go away.

"I'm sorry," Rhode said softly. "I didn't know that she would say those kinds of things. It was just supposed to be a typical reading."

"She told me things that I don't understand," I mumbled, feeling tears form in my eyes again. "She told me things that scared me to death, Rhode, and I don't understand why!"

"Artemis," he breathed, staring at me in a way that I had always feared he would, like I was broken.

"Just take me home," I whispered. "I just want to go home."

"Okay." Rhode nodded. "I'll get you home."

We didn't say a word the entire way home, I just sat in the car, staring out the window as my mind replayed everything that Madame Josephine had said. I told Rhode the truth, I didn't know what she was talking about, but what I hadn't told him was that I could see flashes of the things she was talking about. Things I had never seen with my own eyes, somehow in my memory, as if I had already been there, and then they were just gone. That had been what scared me the most.

Rhode pulled into the driveway of his house, but insisted on walking me back to my place. The house was still dark, which meant no one had noticed I was gone yet, that was a good sign. Rhode and I stood just underneath my window, staring at each other, not knowing what to say now.

"Thank you," I said, breaking the silence. "Thank you for taking me out and letting me experience the real world, even just for a couple of hours. It was really nice."

"Anytime. You're always a welcomed distraction, Artemis Taylor."

I smiled a little, leaning in and kissing him on his cheek, though I had to stand on tiptoes to do it because of his height. "I really hope that I see you tomorrow and that you don't disappear to some military school somewhere."

"So do I, darlin'," he breathed, "but if anyone was worth it, you were."

"Good night, Rhode O'Brian."

"Good morning, Artemis Taylor."

Rhode waited until I had climbed my way into my room, giving me a quick wink before he took off and hopped over the fence to his side. I sat back on my bed, smiling as I relived tonight over and over in my head—tonight really was something else.

"Artemis?" Eris's voice called softly from behind the door.

I didn't answer, closing my eyes when the door opened. I heard soft footsteps cross the room and a blanket being placed over me.

"Good night, little bird," Eris whispered in my ear. "Have the sweetest of dreams." She kissed my forehead before leaving the room, the soft click of my door closing was the only indication that I was alone now.

I curled up underneath the blanket, trying to fall off into the sweet dreams that Eris so desperately wished for me, but Madame Josephine's words swirled around my head and made those dreams impossible.

Chapter 6

The moment I opened my eyes, startled awake by more terrors in the night, I knew something had changed. I didn't know what it was, but I could feel deep in my bones that something had shifted, and I didn't know if that was for the better. That sinking feeling in my gut, coupled with Madame Josephine's words from last night, swirled around my head as I my way down to the kitchen for breakfast.

"We need to tell her," I heard Eris's voice echo down the hall.

"I know," Rhea's voice answered softly. "I'll talk to her soon."

"No." Eris's voice was firm and deadly serious, something I had rarely heard in her voice during my entire life. "Something is coming now and the longer we wait to tell her, the greater danger she's in."

"Okay," Rhea resigned. "I'll tell her this afternoon. Let's just make sure that she's feeling better now. Are you sure that was what she saw?"

"That's what she said and I don't think she could make up those kinds of details. She saw a Reaper."

I blinked in surprise at what Eris had said. A Reaper?

"Shit," Rhea swore softly, the swear echoing in the kitchen followed by a long stretch of silence. "A couple of mornings ago, you were staring up at the sky, Eris. You felt something coming. What's coming?" Rhea asked and, for the first time in my life, I thought I heard fear in her voice.

"Chaos," she said, her voice barely above a whisper and filled with tears.

I slowly made my way to the entrance of the kitchen, peering around it slowly and coming in as if I hadn't heard any part of their conversation. "Morning," I muttered, going to the table and sitting down.

"Morning, little bird," Eris smiled, wiping the tears from her face. "Did you sleep okay?"

"Not really," I answered bluntly.

"Are you feeling up to going to school?" Rhea came over and looked me over closely. "You can stay home if you need another day."

"I'm fine," I said. "My imagination just got the better of me, that's all."

I saw Eris and Rhea exchange a look with each other, but neither of them continued the topic of what had happened to me yesterday. Eris came over and set a plate of eggs and bacon in front of me, placing a hand on top of my head for a moment. "Eat up and I'll drive you to school."

"You never drive me to school," I noted, pushing around my food before taking a small bite.

"I have to open the store today," she explained. "So, I get the pleasure of driving you to school."

I finished my breakfast and Eris and I headed out so she could drop me off for what I was sure was going to be another day of hell and boredom. I noticed as I walked out to the car that the driveway to Rhode's house was empty. I didn't know what it meant, but I couldn't help but feel a sinking feeling in my stomach at the sight of that.

Eris drove me to school in silence; both of us knew there was something we weren't telling the other, we knew each other too well to keep secrets like that. My mind wandered back to what they were talking about in the kitchen this morning, about Reapers and how I was in danger.

My sisters were keeping something big from me, and I knew it was the mother of all secrets.

After the crazy couple of days I'd had at school, I really wanted one day where I was just the invisible new girl. I didn't think that was too much to ask for, but of course The Rolling Stones said it best, you can't always get what you want.

The moment I walked through the front doors, all eyes were on me, staring at me like I had a neon arrow over my head. I could see guys staring at me and laughing with their buddies and girls giggling and whispering, smirking with laughter. Pointing and laughing at the freak.

I couldn't even make it to my first class before it become too much. I just stood there in the hall as everyone pointed and laughed and gossiped about rumors that probably weren't even true to begin with. I could feel my chest tighten and I almost thought I was going to have a panic attack right there in front of the whole school. Wouldn't that be a sight?

I closed my eyes as I felt a familiar hand slip into mine. "Just ignore them," Rhode whispered in my ear. "Something else will happen and you'll be yesterday's news."

I opened my eyes and looked at Rhode, who stood there with that cocky grin of his on his face. "I thought you would have been on your way to get a really bad haircut by now." I laughed nervously.

"Nah," Rhode said, "I told you that he wasn't going to send me anywhere." He fell off and I noticed a black eye on the other side of his face. "He does, however, believe in tough love."

I reached out and brushed my fingertips against it. "Jesus."

"Not the first time it's happened," Rhode shrugged, "sure as hell won't be the last."

"You get a kick out of pissing your brother off, don't you?" I asked, noticing a small bit of pride in his voice. "Or are you just a masochist?"

Rhode took a quick moment, as if he were weighing the answer in his head. "80/20," he answered. He offered me his arms. "Shall we go to class?"

"Yeah." I sighed, taking it. "Why the fuck not?"

I honestly didn't foresee the day going at all well, and given the stares throughout math class, I decided to take the high road and ignore every single person I came into contact with during the day. Expect maybe Rhode. What I hadn't calculated in my plan was the ever-persistent Caleb was in second period French with me.

"Good morning, beautiful." Caleb smiled as he took his seat next to me.

I lifted my head out of my book for a small moment to assure Caleb that I was not deaf before returning to it to assure him that I was ignoring him.

"*A Scanner Darkly*," he noted, seeing my book. "Interesting choice."

It wasn't an interesting choice so much as a foreshadow of very slowly losing my mind without realizing I was actually doing it. Phillip K. Dick liked to remind the world that we were all slowly going mad and I decided that if I were, I was going in head first.

"Please don't ignore me," Caleb pleaded. "I don't think you're a freak, Artemis."

"Seeing you point and snicker with your friends this morning doesn't exactly invoke confidence in that statement, Caleb," I said bitterly, nose still buried in my paperback.

"Come on, I like you, I wouldn't do anything to hurt your feelings."

"Please refer to the previous statement."

"Fine, why don't I show you rather than tell you," he said, still standing firm on talking to me. "A bunch of us are going to be at the bayou tonight, why don't you come and join us? There will be free beer and there's bound to be something way more embarrassing happen than what you think happened to you yesterday. You'll be yesterday's news by first period tomorrow, I promise."

"I'll pass, thanks," I said, unable to keep the bitterness about of my voice.

"Just think about it," Caleb insisted. "I think you'll have a good time."

After spending the day ignoring the entire existence of my peers, Rhode walked me home. We walked in silence, not because we didn't have anything to say to each other, but I think it was because we liked those moments. Small splices of time where it was silence and no one else; I think Rhode was the only one who got that, and maybe that was one of the reasons we clicked.

We reached my house first and just stood on the sidewalk, neither of us knowing what to say to the other or even whether to say it. I made the first move. I turned to look at him and a smile formed on my face. I gestured toward the backyard and backed slowly toward the gate.

I walked over to my archery set up and started shooting at the target without a word to Rhode, who just stood watching me for a pregnant moment.

"You really are good at this stuff," he said, finally breaking the silence.

"My mom told me when I was little that when I was born she had a feeling that I would be a good shot. So, she named me after the goddess of the hunt, Artemis. Said that it was in my blood," I explained, drawing back and letting another arrow fly. "It does help that I'm picturing Caleb's head as the target."

"Has he been bothering you?"

"I could say the same thing about you," I said with a shrug. "He's a guy, it's nothing that I can't handle. Trust me on that."

"Have you ever hit a moving target before?" he asked, looking at me with a smirk.

"Wouldn't you like to know?"

"What's going on in your head, Artemis?" Rhode asked, his turn to make his move. "You seemed so quiet today but I can see the wheels in your head turning."

"I think my sisters are keeping a secret from me," I said, honestly. "I think they know more than they're telling."

"About what?"

I looked at him for a long moment. "About everything."

"Artemis," Rhea called as she came out the backdoor and into the yard.

Rhode stood up and put on his gentlemanly disguise. "How are you doing today, Rhea?"

Rhea, of course, did the same thing in return. "I'm fine, Rhode. I just need to talk to Artemis about some personal things. You understand, don't you?"

"Of course. I should get going before my brother comes looking for me." He turned his gaze on me. "I'll see you in class tomorrow?"

"Sure," I said, not being able to keep myself from smiling.

Rhode gave me a wink before he ran to the fence, hopping over it into the next yard as Rhea and I watched him. I stood there, quietly waiting for Rhea to smother me with questions about my day or if I were alright or ream me out for bringing a stranger to the house without her or Eris being home.

"Come sit with me," she said so softly that I was a bit shocked. Rhea walked to the middle of the yard, sitting on a patch of grass before she beckoned me to come sit with her.

I moved slowly to where she was, sitting across from her as she took my hand into hers. "Mom used to do this with me right before she told me that we were moving again."

Rhea's only response was a nod before she tilted her head back and looked up at the sky, allowing the sun to bask on her face for a long moment. I could have sworn that I saw her smile when she did this.

"What are you hiding from me, Ray?"

"This wasn't something we were hiding from you. It was something we were going to sit down as a family and talk about. Then the accident happened and Eris and I decided to let you recover from losing Mom before we dropped all of this on you."

I blinked at her, completely lost by what was going on right now. "You're scaring me, Ray. What are you talking about?"

Rhea sighed, her eyes holding sadness as she looked at me. "I think it'll be better if I show you."

Before I could ask what she was talking about, Rhea closed her eyes and gripped my hands in hers. Around us the entire yard started to move; the grass around us became greener and soon flowers surfaced from beneath the Earth. I looked around, seeing wildflowers of blue, purple, pink, red, and white swarm around us.

Rhea opened her eyes and looked at me. "You're a witch, Artemis. Descended from a long line of powerful witches that goes all the way back to Salem. Do you remember the elements?"

I nodded numbly as I looked around, too stunned by what I had seen to speak, and even if the power of speech hadn't escaped me at that moment, I had no idea what it was I would have said.

"Fire, water, earth, air, and spirit," Rhea said for me. "Each witch has an affinity to an element in this world. Mom was a water witch, Eris is an air witch, and I'm an earth witch."

"What am I supposed to be?" My lips barely moved as I spoke.

Rhea just shook her head. "I don't know. A witch's affinity presents itself at different times. I didn't know what mine was until I was eighteen."

"Why are you telling me all this now?"

"Mom was going to tell you before you moved in with us. We were going to talk about it together and then you were going to learn from Eris and I while you finished high school. Then the accident happened . . ."

I pulled my hands from hers and wiped away a tear that rolled down my cheek. I hadn't recalled tears forming. "This can't be real," I breathed numbly.

"It can't, but it is. It is real and it is what we are as a family."

"A witch?"

Rhea reached out and brushed the hair away from my face as more tears I was too numb to notice started pouring down my face. "Yes, and I'm sorry honey, I wish that I could have found a better way to sit down and tell you. You need to know this now, because something is coming."

"What do you mean?" I asked. "What's coming?"

"I don't know, but its powerful enough to put all of us in danger. We can't have you in the dark anymore."

Rhea stood up, brushing herself off before she offered her hand out to me. When I didn't take it, she knelt down and looked me in the eye. "I know this is a lot to take in, and right now I won't push you, but I need you to know that this is real and this is important."

I looked at her, my mind going a million miles a minute and nothing sticking. Rhea wiped the tears from my cheek and took my hand, helping me up. "Let's go inside," she said, allowing my weight to lean against hers as we walked. "Eris is making cookies."

Eris was pulling a tray of cookies out of the oven and setting them on a cooling rack as Rhea and I came into the kitchen. She looked up as we came in and immediately knew what had happened. "Did you tell her?"

"That we're a family of fucking witches?" I said bitterly as I walked numbly to the kitchen table and sat down with a hard thump. "Yeah, that bomb got dropped."

Eris came over with a plate of cookies that had already cooled, placing them on the table in front of me. She pulled one of the chairs up close to me and sat down. "I'm so sorry that you had to find out like this, little bird."

I looked over at Rhea, but she was standing by the window watching Rhode's house like a hawk. "I want you to steer clear of the new neighbors until we can decide what's what."

"What are you talking about?" My outrage snapped me out of the numb state I had been in. "Rhode is the only friend I have, why would I avoid him?"

"I just want to get a vibe for them before everyone gets chummy."

Eris, being the buffer that she has always been, stepped in on my behalf. "Ray, we can't isolate ourselves from everyone because you think they're coming after Artemis?"

The last part had put me off guard. "What are you talking about? Who's after me?"

Rhea looked straight at Eris, both of them ignoring my question. "I wouldn't be able to forgive myself if something happened to her," she said slowly in a low tone.

"We can trust Rhode," I interjected. "I can feel it in my bones."

Rhea gave me a look, something I couldn't put my name on. Eris pushed the plate of cookies closer to me. "Let's not talk about such negative things right now," she said softly, casting a look at Rhea. "Tell me about your day at school, Artemis."

"What, like we're a normal fucking family and I didn't have everything I knew for seventeen years just ripped apart five minutes ago?"

"Yes, because despite what you just learned and how you feel, I am still your sister and I still love you. Now eat a cookie and tell me about your day."

I decided to forgo being a social pariah for the day in hopes that all of this would pass, choosing to start with a lighter subject. "I meet this guy, Caleb, he's in my French class." I paused there, watching Rhea's expression to see if she would rile up again. When she remained neutral, I continued. "He invited me to a party tonight."

"Absolutely not," Rhea said evenly, no note of anger or irritation in her voice.

Eris, always my advocate, came in to my rescue. "Come on Rhea, it's a party, not the end of the world."

Rhea turned and looked at me. "I'm really glad you're back in the world again, Artemis, because after the last year I thought I was going to lose you. If things were a little different, if we were just a little more normal, then this wouldn't be an issue."

"Only things aren't different and we are far from normal," I noted.

"This is an issue that I'm going to have to stand firm on," she said firmly. "I want to be your older sister and to help you have fun and flourish in this world, but I'm also responsible for keeping you in it."

I paused for a moment, knowing that I had two options here, I could cause a fuss and not get my way, or I could concede and if I conceded there was a way for me to get something out of it. "Let me hang out with Rhode and I'll let it go," I said.

Rhea sighed and, after a moment, said, "Fine. You can hang out with Rhode, but be careful, we still don't know what's going on yet."

Chapter 7

After dinner, I was sitting on my bed, reading for English class as I waited for Rhode to push his brother further and come knock on my window when my phone rang. That was definitely more than strange because I hadn't had this number but a year and I hadn't even given it to anyone yet, not even Rhode.

"Hello?"

"Hello, beautiful." I heard a smooth voice on the other line that I had only heard for the first time just this morning.

"Caleb," I said. "How did you get my number?"

"I've got my ways, Artemis."

"You do realize that's what serial killers say, right? Last I checked, I don't hang out with serial killers."

"I looked you up in the student directory," Caleb explained, "but that kind of sounds lame."

"Yeah, girls really dig the Patrick Bateman kind of vibe now."

"Duly noted."

I could tell that I had deflated his ego a little. "What do you want?"

"Are you coming to my party tonight?"

I marked my place in the book and set it aside. "Your party?"

"Well, it's a team party, so it's kind of mine by association," he explained. "So, are you coming?"

I got up and paced to the window quietly. Looking out into Rhode's backyard, I could see him on the back porch arguing with someone who I could only assume was his brother. I cracked the window as I tried to listen in on what they were saying.

"We're here for a reason, Rhode, and it isn't so that you can get your dick wet," his brother said sternly, sizing up Rhode, but Rhode refused to move from where he was standing.

"It's not like that," he countered. "Artemis and I are just friends."

"Last I checked, you don't go crawling into your friend's windows in the middle of the night," his brother spat. "Get your head in the game, little brother, because this is bigger than all of us."

They finished whatever conversation they were having and Rhode walked off into the yard, clearly agitated. He pulled out a cigarette from behind his ear and began to smoke it.

"I can't," I said to Caleb, my mind remembering that I was having a conversation with him. "I'm sort of on lockdown, tonight."

"Fuck that, come anyway."

"You have obviously never seen my sisters when they're cross with me," I said, still watching Rhode as he smoked, oblivious to me as I did so.

"Cross? What are you, Mary Poppins now?"

"Sorry," I said softly, forgetting that I was back stateside and not to use slang, but living in Europe for most of my life, the slang stuck around even if the accents didn't.

"Well, you should still come any way. I think it might be worth your sister getting cross with you." I could hear the humor in his voice at using the word.

"Caleb—" I said softly, preparing to shut him down again and hold up my end of the deal with Rhea and let the party go.

"I'll text you the address," he interrupted. "I'll be looking for you." He hung up before I could say anything else and, less than a minute later, my phone chimed with a message that contained the address of the party.

I stood stunned for a moment, thinking about what to do before I finally said fuck it and went into my closet. I changed into a clean pair of jeans, a red halter top, and a pair of beat up red converse, opting to pull my hair back into a ponytail in lieu of trying to brush it.

One of the perks that had come with being a shut-in for as long as I had was having knowledgeable of the layout of the house to a tee, and tonight that knowledge came in handy. My far window opened onto the roof and was in reach of the tree that belonged to the neighboring yard.

Rhode had finished smoking his cigarette and was just staring at the sky now as I landed in the grass behind him with a soft thud. The sound caught his attention as he turned around with a start. "Holy shit!"

"Quiet," I said in a hushed voice, "are you trying to wake up my sisters?"

"Sorry, what are you doing out here?"

I ignored the question and gestured to the pack of cigarettes in his hand. "You got anything stronger than tobacco? I've had a shit day."

Rhode took a moment to look back at the house to make sure we were alone before he reached into the cigarette pack and pulled out a joint. He looked at me with a Cheshire Cat smile as he put it between his lips, lighting it and taking a puff. He held the joint out to me and I came closer, taking it from him.

Rhode lay back on the grass, looking up at the stars, and I did the same, taking another puff before I passed it to him. "I used to look up at the stars with my mother," I said absently, watching the stars as they twinkled against their dark backdrop. "At least when we were in places where the lights weren't so bright and we could see them."

"My mother and I did the same thing," Rhode said softly. "She used to take me to the woods and we'd map the constellations." He turned his head to look at me but I kept staring at the stars. "What'll your sisters say if they catch you out here getting high with the neighbor kid?" He passed me the joint.

"They would be upset but not surprised," I muttered, taking a puff and turning my head to look at him as I passed him back the joint. "My nickname when I lived in London was Alice."

"As in, Go *Ask Alice?*"

"As in, 'Down the rabbit hole.'" I said. "Trust me, pot is not the drug they're concerned with me partaking in." I sat up and leaned over, giving Rhode a kiss on the cheek before I stood up off the ground and dusted myself off. "Thanks for getting me high. Enjoy the roach, I've got a party to get to."

"Where?" he asked in surprise. "You don't know anyone."

I flipped him off at that remark, but all he did was smile at the gesture. "Caleb invited me to a party in the bayou."

"I take it by the Mission Impossible stunts into my yard that your sisters don't want you to go." I had to hand it to him, the boy wasn't stupid.

"Gold star," I chuckled. "Figured I'd try some teenage rebellion."

"I don't think that it's a good idea to go," Rhode said slowly, getting up off the grass. "You don't know anyone. It's dark and it isn't safe."

"Okay," I said, looking him up and down, not sure what I was looking for. "Why don't you come with me if you're so concerned about my safety?"

Rhode stared at me for a moment. I knew he wasn't going to let me go alone, but I allowed him to pretend that he had to think about it. "Shall we?" he asked.

———◆▸✕◂◆———

THE PARTY WAS in a wooded bayou that looked almost like another world compared to where we had just come from. The place was thick with students from not only my high school but schools all over New Orleans, sprinkled with college kids selling drugs. There was a large bonfire set up in the center of the party and music booming all around as if no one cared about anyone hearing it and calling the cops.

"Are you sure you want to waste your teenage rebellion on this?" Rhode asked once we arrived. We had shared a taxi rather than hoof it the entire trip.

"You're the one who started all this," I said, taking a Jell-O shot from a pink-haired girl who passed us by. "I want to feel like a teenager again, even if it's just a lie that I have to tell myself to make me happy sometimes."

"What happened?" Rhode asked, clearly caught off guard by what I said. "What did Rhea say to you this afternoon? What did she tell you?"

I looked him dead in the eye and said evenly, "She ripped my world apart."

I didn't wait for his response before walking into the throws of the party, feeling every vibration of the music fill me as I remembered the days when I would sneak out of the house with my mates from whatever country or town I was in at the time. A real feeling of normalcy rushed over me and suddenly, I wasn't broken Artemis Taylor, the girl whose mother died, I was Artemis, the life of the whole fucking party.

"You made it!" Caleb's voice came over the music.

I took the red cup he gave me as I looked around at the party in amazement. "This is awesome!"

"I'm so glad that the great Artemis Taylor approves." He looked around for a moment before pulling two little yellow pills out of his pocket. Our eyes met and I could see the intensity beaming in his deep brown eyes. "You want to have some real fun?"

I looked down at the pills then back at him, feeling myself creep up to a line and wondering whether I should cross it. I knew the dangers of being out here with a bunch of strangers without Rhea or Eris knowing where I was, and I knew the dangers of taking pills from a guy I had known for less than twenty-four hours, but for some reason, in that moment, it all didn't seem to matter.

"What is it?" I looked at the little yellow pill and saw a black imprint of a kitty on it. "Doesn't look like anything I've seen before."

"It's new, my buddy gave it to me last week. He guaranteed me that it would be the best high of your life."

"Fuck it." I threw all caution and common sense to the wind as I picked up the pill and placed it in my mouth, chasing it down with a shallow of beer. "Down the rabbit hole."

———◆◆◆———

I DIDN'T KNOW where I was or how much time had passed, but I could remember someone calling my name over and over again. I didn't say anything, though, I was lost and floating and unaware of the world that was above me or below me, at that point I really didn't know.

"I always worried that my mom would send me away one day," I said to no one in particular. I didn't even know if anyone was actually listening. "You know, she's sick of dragging a kid all over the world and one day she'd send me to live with some relatives or something." I giggled at that, half because of the drugs and half because Mom had not a relative to speak of to even send me to. "Then she drops the bomb that I'm going to New Orleans to live with my sisters and that it's for the best right now.

"A couple of days before I'm supposed to leave, she takes me to the park to stargaze like we used to when I was younger. She points up at the moon and tells me that whenever I feel lonely in the world I should look up at the moon and know that her and my sisters were looking at the same moon and, that in knowing that, I would never be alone. Only I feel more alone than ever right now."

I closed my eyes and let the high take me back up to whatever or wherever I was that made me so fucking happy. I broke the surface as I heard my name being called over and over by a voice that I felt this strange attraction to. There was something so safe and familiar about that voice.

"Artemis!" Rhode called again, snapping me back to the world that I had clearly checked out of.

I looked around, completely unaware of where I was or how long I had been there. I was sitting around the fire, leaning against Caleb who wasn't as lost as I had just been. Had he been the one I was talking to? I didn't know, I couldn't even remember what I had said to him or if it was even him I had talked to.

I looked up at Rhode, who was staring down at me with a mix of anger and concern on his face. "Rhode," I said with a stupid smile on my face. "Hi."

"Yes, you most definitely are," he said in a low tone. He reached down to help me to my feet. "Come on, we need to get out of here."

"No," I groaned, scooting closer to Caleb.

"Come on, Artemis, it's one in the fucking morning. You're drunk and you're high, we need to get you home so you can sleep this off."

"The lady says that she doesn't want to go," Caleb said in a deep, level voice. "Leave her be."

"Fine," he said, tossing his hands up in surrender or defeat, in that moment I couldn't tell. "Do whatever the fuck you like, I'm going home."

I watched him walk off with the strong feeling that I should get up and go after him or tell him to come back and take me home. Only problem was that I was another person and that person didn't want to go home, she wanted to get obliterated by the world. She had taken over me at the moment and she was going to get exactly what she wanted.

Caleb moved to the side before standing up. I didn't have the mental capacity to stay up on my own so I fell over onto my side, staring at the fire with laser focus. "Come on," Caleb said, as I rolled over onto my back and looked at him as he offered me his hand.

I took it and he pulled me off the ground, keeping his hold on my hand as he dragged me deeper into the woods. We walked farther and farther and farther until the fire from the party was a tiny flicker in the side of my vision and the music was nonexistent. I could finally hear myself think for the first time in hours.

Caleb pushed me up against one of the trees, kissing me and he lifting one of my legs as he started caressing me. "I want you," he said in a savage voice. "I want you so much it fucking hurts. Whoa."

"What?" I lifted my head to look at him.

He smiled and shook his head. "Nothing, it just looked like . . . For a minute, it looked like your eyes were glowing."

"I bet you say that to all the girls." I giggled as Caleb's mouth roamed lower and lower down my neck.

My head fell back against the tree as waves of pleasure washed over me. I was almost lost to the world when I heard the snap of a tree branch and leaves rustle. That sound brought me all the way back to reality and, for a moment, I hated myself as the events tonight became very real. "Did you hear that?" I pushed Caleb away from me as my survival mode kicked in, pushing away the haze of the drugs and the alcohol that had led me to this vulnerable position in the first place.

"Shh," Caleb whispered as he continued probing my body.

The noise came again and I pushed Caleb fully off me, pulling out a knife from where I had hidden it inside my boot. "Alright perv, show's over."

The rustling came from all directions now as I struggled to see into the dark as figures emerged from the shadows. Caleb and I watched as a dozen men in white masks and long black coats came out of the trees toward us. My heart started pounding as they reminded me of the figure in class.

"What the fuck?" Caleb breathed, having no clue what we faced.

I knew what they were, and I was more terrified than I had ever been in my life. Even if I didn't know what they were consciously, deep down in my gut, I knew. From the bedtime stories Mom used to tell me at night to what I saw that day in history class. I immediately recognized the greatest danger there was to me, now and in the future.

Reapers.

That recognition immediately sobered me from whatever high I had been enjoying.

"Run," I whispered to Caleb, knowing I would never be able to fight off this many of them.

"What?"

"Run!" I pushed him in the opposite direction as the one I headed off in. It was a stupid idea to run—I had no clue of the landscape and it was pitch black—but I had no other options that I could think of.

The stupidity made itself clear as I was slammed against a tree so hard my breath was knocked out of me. It wouldn't have mattered anyway, because the second I came face to face with the white-masked Reapers, I couldn't think to breathe.

I had only heard about Reapers in bedtime stories my mother used to tell me when I was too young to take things seriously. Mom would tell me stories about battles between witches that fought for good and to protect the world and the Reapers that fought for their own greed and sought to destroy the world and every witch inhabiting it. In her stories, Mom said no witch had ever come face to face with a Reaper and lived to tell the tale, but they gave their lives in service of all that was good. The Reapers wanted to eradicate all witches—my kind. To cleanse the earth of witches was their sole purpose in life.

All those stories came crashing back to me as I realized they were not the result of an overactive imagination. Everything she told me was real.

I knew in that moment I was going to die tonight.

"Artemis," the Reaper said darkly behind his mask.

I was breathing in scattered, shaky breaths, trying to control my faculties so I didn't piss myself in front of him. I wouldn't give him the satisfaction of knowing I was scared.

"H-h-how do y-y-you know my n-n-name?"

"You should have perished with your mother." His bright blue eyes looked at me behind his mask as if with curiosity. "Fear not, we have plans far greater for you than death."

I didn't ask him what he meant by that, because it wouldn't have been good. The only time a Reaper would have wanted to keep a witch alive was when what he had intended was awful enough to make the witch wish she had been killed.

I wasn't going to let that happen. I jammed my knife into his gut and twisted it, pushing him off and letting him fall to the ground and writhe in pain as I fled, running faster than I ever thought I had in my life. I nearly screamed when I ran into something else.

I fought against it with everything I had. I didn't care what I had to do to survive tonight, but I was not going to fucking die.

"Shh," the voice said, "it's me, Artemis."

I stopped fighting and nearly went limp with relief in his Rhode's arms. "Rhode," I cried gratefully, putting my arms around him as he pulled me into a hug.

"Come on, the road isn't far from here." He put his arm around my waist as we walked through the woods, neither of us saying anything until we reached the road.

"How far are we from home?" I looked around the empty streets, scratching off any chance of catching a cab.

Rhode shook his head as he looked up and down the dark road. "Not sure. I called for a ride, but we're going to have to walk a bit."

"Okay." My words were calm, but I couldn't keep my hands or my voice from shaking.

Rhode looked at me and I'm sure he saw the mess that I looked, inside and out. Even though it was the last thing I wanted from him, he took pity on me. "Come on," he said, signaling for me to get onto his back. He turned around and crouched to the ground so I could straddle his back. He counted to three before standing upright, hooking his arms around my legs as I looped my arms around his neck gently, resting my ear against his back so I could hear his breathing and his heart beat as he started walking down the road.

"Who'd you call?" I asked sleepily as the pills continued to work and the last of the adrenaline faded from my system in the pitch blackness of the night.

"I called my brother, Tennessee." He hoisted me higher onto his back. "Needless to say that he's pretty pissed at me for sneaking off again, but I needed to get you home safe."

"Tennessee," I said numbly, "like the state."

"He was actually named after Tennessee Williams. I was named after the state."

I lifted my head up and rested my chin on his shoulder, watching for a moment or two as he walked with only the moon and stars to guide him through the dark. "Thank you," I said into his ear as I leaned into him, tightening my grip around his neck a little, "for coming back for me."

Rhode didn't answer my question, and I was sure that he hadn't heard what I'd said. He carried me in silence after that, neither one of us attempting to speak to the other until a pair of headlights appeared down the dark road. The lights flashed on and off three times, almost as if it were a type of pattern.

"That's our ride," he said, stopping and letting me slide off his back.

I was mostly sober now and able to hold myself up steadily. The car stopped just short of where we stood, but I was still ready to flee at any sign of trouble. I saw Tennessee get out of the driver's side of the car, followed by Rhea getting out of the passenger side. I froze the moment I saw my oldest sister, unsure if I should flee.

Rhea got out and walked closer to me, and I could see the anger in her face. No, not really anger, it was more of a worried kind of anguish. That was something I hadn't seen on Rhea's face since after the accident, but back then I had been too out to lunch to register it. Now, I was all too aware of that look and it broke my heart to see it on her face.

"Ray, I'm sorry," I tried to spit out, but Rhea didn't say a thing.

She came up to me in a rush and gathered me up in a tight hug. "Don't you ever do that to me again," she said in a broken voice so low that only I could hear her.

———————

"DO YOU KNOW how stupid you were?" Rhea asked as we sat in the kitchen.

I sat at the table, staring down, too embarrassed to meet her eyes while Rhode and Tennessee stood off to the side of the kitchen near the threshold of the living room, allowing us to have a private moment. That moment had gone on for a good ten minutes. Rhea was grateful I was okay the entire way home, but the moment the door had shut behind us after we got back Rhea had flipped her switch and completely lost it on me. It wasn't as if I didn't deserve it.

Eris set a large glass of water in front of me. "Drink this. You need to stay hydrated, you'll thank me in the morning when you're sober," she said with a humorless smile.

I took a long sip to appease her. I've had some record-breaking hangovers, and I had a feeling that I could handle the one that was coming in the morning. Lord knew I deserved it for how I'd acted tonight.

"You snuck out and went to a party in the middle of nowhere where you proceeded to get high and drunk to the point where anything could have happened to you!" Rhea gasped, frustrated by my thinking, or lack thereof.

"Lighten up on her, Ray," Eris stepped in, defending me for the time being. "She's just had a lot of information loaded on her. She just wanted to let off a little steam."

"You are lucky that Rhode had the sense to call us when you refused to leave the party," Rhea said, her tone calming down now that she had run out of steam, but she still wasn't done with me yet.

"Ray . . ." I breathed as the events of tonight became so real to me and I couldn't fight the emotions that were starting to bubble the surface. Rhea stopped her rant and looked at me, seeing the seriousness in my face. "I wasn't alone in those woods tonight."

"What?" Eris and Rhea's voice asked in unison, their eyes concentrated on me.

"There were Reapers in those woods tonight," Rhode said behind us, "a dozen of them, at least. It's the largest group I've ever seen in one place."

Rhea froze at the news of the Reapers, but I turned to looked at Rhode; he stood behind us with a stone-cold expression, and his brother stood next to him with the same one. "They know about us," I breathed, scrambling off my chair and circling around the island as I pulled a kitchen knife from the knife block on the counter.

"Calm down, little witch," Tennessee said, his Irish accent almost making his words move slower and calmer from his mouth. Neither he nor Rhode moved toward me or my sisters as we stood around the kitchen, staring at each other as if someone were waiting for someone to do something.

"Is that why you were hanging around me?" I asked with hurt in my voice as I pointed the knife at Rhode. "Is that why you pretended to be my friend? Is that why you live next door?"

"How do we know that the Reaper attacks and the two of you showing up aren't related?" Rhea asked in a stony voice. She was so close that I could feel the warmth of her magic come off of her as she summoned it.

"That's because they are," Rhode said. "All those Reapers are here for one reason. Artemis."

"We were sent by the Elders to protect the girl," Tennessee said, motioning toward me.

"Prove it," I said.

Tennessee came up to me slowly, but I refused to lower the knife as he approached. He stopped just short of my swing zone. He pulled off a medallion from around his neck and tossed it to me. I caught and looked at the little silver medal with a raven on it. I held it out for Rhea who took it and looked it over with calm eyes. "What does it mean?"

"I thought the O'Brian witches died out," she said quietly.

"Nearly," Tennessee said in a low voice. "Reapers killed our mother ten years ago while we were living in Dublin. I was only fifteen when it happened, so I did the only thing I could think to do. I grabbed my brother and we fled Ireland, came to the States and went into hiding. We were living in Alaska up until a few months ago when we were summoned by the Elders. They ordered us to protect the Taylor witches. Artemis is particular."

"Why?" Eris bit out from the table. I had forgotten for a moment she was sitting there until she spoke, getting up from the table to stand next to me, her hand resting gently on my shoulder. "Put the knife down, little bird," she coaxed, "they won't hurt us. They're Guardians."

"Is that supposed to make me feel better?"

"Guardians are the highest form of protection a witch can be given," Eris explained. "The Elders wouldn't have sent them to protect us if they weren't powerful enough to hold off the threats the Elders think are coming."

My mind flashed back to what Madame Josephine had told me that night in the Quarter. Warriors that have come to protect me. Slowly, I allowed Eris to lower my arm and take the knife from my hand as I watched Tennessee and Rhode, who weren't moving from their spots. They didn't want us to see them as a threat.

"The accident you told me about wasn't an accident. Your car was run off the road by Reapers," Rhode said softly.

"What?" I asked, feeling like I had been punched in the gut. "Are you telling me that my mother was murdered?"

"You were meant to die with her," Rhode continued. "The Reapers meant to kill you both."

"Only I survived."

"Only you survived," he affirmed. "Not long after that the rumors of your magic started spreading and the Elders felt the Reapers were going to make a bigger move."

"That's why he said it," I realized, numbly.

"Said what?" Rhea asked, her full attention on me now.

"There was a Reaper in the woods," I breathed. "He pinned me against the tree and told me that I should have died with Mom, but now the Reapers had greater plans for me than death."

"You were face to face with a Reaper?" Tennessee asked. I could hear the concern in his voice, but there was no hiding the thinly veiled anger there as well. "When was this?"

"Right before I ran into Rhode. I stabbed him and took off. I'm not even sure if he's dead or not."

"We'll go back to the woods and check." Tennessee's eyes shifted to Rhode, who had suddenly gone tense and quiet. Tennessee went over to him, clasping him by the back of the neck and saying sternly in his ear, "You need to step outside now, little brother."

Rhode nodded, heading straight out the backdoor without a word from anyone. He left the door open behind him and I ran after him. He walked until he reached the middle of the yard, staring up at the sky as he kept rolling his shoulders as if he was agitated.

I could feel Tennessee's strong presence beside me, as well as my sisters, all of us standing there and watching as Rhode finally stilled, his eyes still watching the stars. "Rhode," I breathed, my eyes locked on to him as he dropped to his knees and doubled over in pain.

I was about to take a step forward when I felt Eris's grip tighten around me as she pulled me closer to her. "No, stay back."

In a flash of white light Rhode had disappeared and, in his place, was a large wolf that emerged from the clothes Rhode had been wearing. I looked at the wolf, mesmerized by his dark gray fur and toffee-colored eyes that were identical to Rhode's.

"Whoa," I breathed.

"Shifter," Rhea said, equally amazed as I was. "I've never met one before."

"He's a spirit witch as well," Tennessee said, keeping a hold on the wolf as he looked around, adjusting to his new surroundings. "His Gift gives him better control of his ability to change than most Shifters, but emotional distress can trigger an involuntary shift. We're still working on that," he added with a heavy sigh.

I took a step forward toward the wolf, his eyes locking onto mine.

"No, don't," Eris said urgently.

I ignored her, walking slowly toward the wolf until I reached him. I sank down onto my knees and we stared at each other, like our souls were having a conversation. The wolf blinked and leaned forward, licking my face as if we had known each other all our lives. "Good boy." I chuckled, ruffling his ears gently.

"I've never seen a half Shifter, half witch before," Rhea said evenly.

"It's rarer than rare," Tennessee affirmed. "Our mother was a spirit witch and our father a Shifter. Rhode and I both inherited her magic, but Rhode also inherited our father's shifter genes."

"Why didn't you?" Eris asked curiously.

Tennessee just shrugged. "I believe it's because my magic is more powerful than Rhode's, or maybe it's because he would need someone to guide him through this as he gained control of his Gift."

"What's your Gift?" Eris asked.

"I'm a healer," Tennessee said simply, looking down at me as I interacted with Rhode's wolf.

I had sunk down to the ground and lay on my side, feeling the soft grass underneath me as I looked up at the stars, Rhode's wolf lying down beside me protectively. He rested his head on my stomach and I petted him gently on his head as we just lie there.

"I think it's time to let you get some sleep, little witch," Tennessee said gently as he walked over to where I lay in the yard and picked me up in his strong arms, carrying me back into the house and up to my room as my sisters followed behind.

Tennessee settled me into my bed and I looked at him as he reached out to touch my face. He looked at me for a long moment, and I think in that moment he saw the fear that was in my eyes that I had been trying to hide since that day in history class.

"You're safe now, little witch," he said softly. "My brother and I are here to protect you."

I looked up into his stormy brown eyes, seeing small flecks of amber in them. "It's all going to end very badly," I breathed in a low voice, unaware of what I was saying or that my lips were even moving. "There's a fire and it's all going to burn."

"Artemis." Rhea's voice came from the doorway, concern overpowering her voice as she came over to be. "What are you talking about?"

"She's still high," Tennessee said with a small but humorless smile. Only I could see in his eyes that he didn't believe that. He kissed my forehead and whispered, "Go to sleep, little witch. Have good dreams."

He stood up off the bed and turned to my sisters. "I'll take Rhode back home and see if I can get him to shift back so we can check the woods. See if that Reaper is still out there."

"Thank you for your help," Eris said. "Please be careful out there."

Tennessee nodded to her in acknowledgment before he left the room.

"I'll see him out," Rhea said in a soft voice. "Can you make sure she's alright?"

"Of course," Eris said gently.

My adrenaline was gone and I was numb and too drained to move from the spot on my bed where I had been deposited. Eris came over to the bed and covered me with the comforter before she sat down on the bed with me, stoking my hair as she waited for me to drop off to sleep.

"I just wanted to be normal again. After all this, just for one night I wanted to go back to before I knew," I mumbled, feeling my high crashing rapidly and my eyes becoming impossible to keep open.

"I know, honey. After Mom and Rhea told me, my reaction wasn't much different than yours. Rhea knows that. She's just being hard on you because she's scared."

"I'm scared too, Chaos," I whispered, calling her the nickname she had when we were little girls, remembering the blonde tornado of energy that Eris had been in what felt like another lifetime to me.

"Sleep tight, little bird," she whispered, kneeling down and kissing my cheek.

I was out before she left the room.

Chapter 8

I knew from the second I opened my eyes that I wasn't awake. At least not completely. I was in a room, a brick basement of some sort, without any windows and only one large steel door on the other end of the room. I watched from the corner as a boy that looked no older than myself lay on his side on the floor, beaten and bloody, shivering from the chill in the room.

I jumped as the steel door creaked opened, going farther into my corner as two men, both dressed identical to the men I saw in the woods, came walking into the room. The first man that got to him kicked the boy in the gut and I flinched as I could hear the bones in his body break.

"I told you where they were," the boy stammered in. "I told you where you could find the girl, please let me go."

The man that kicked him knelt over the boy. "You didn't tell us that there were Guardians sent to protect the girl."

"I didn't know! I did what you told me, I found the Taylor witches and I made sure that you knew where to find the girl. I didn't know about the Guardians!"

"It doesn't matter now," the man said, righting himself and stepping aside, allowing another Reaper to step through. His steps were slow and I noticed he was holding his side. "You're no longer useful to us."

"No," the boy pleaded as the temperature in the room seemed to drop at least ten degrees and kept falling drastically until I could see his scared breaths hanging in the air. "No, please. Don't kill me."

The Reaper stood over the boy. "Shh," he whispered. "It will only hurt for a moment. You've earned a quick death." He pulled out a long hunting knife and plunged it into the boy, staring at him with emotionless eyes as the men watched the life fade from his body.

I sat up in my bed, screaming bloody murder before I realized I was even awake. The door burst open and Eris came into the room, coming over to the bed and wrapping me up in her arms like she had done dozens of times before when I had screamed myself awake.

"Shh, shh," she whispered in my ear, holding me as tight as she could to keep me from flailing around. "Look at me, Artemis, look at me."

It took everything I had to stop screaming. My breathing was shaky and uneven as Eris's face came into view. It had all been a dream.

No. A nightmare.

The sound of a wolf howling made me flinch before a dull recollection came that it must have been Rhode's wolf. Eris kept her arms around me as I continued to try and calm myself back down. I looked over her shoulder to see Rhea was standing in the doorway talking quietly on the phone.

"No, don't come over, it's still dark."

She paused to listen.

"If you think it will settle him down. We can't have the neighbors calling the cops about wolves on the loose, it'll draw too much attention to us, and we don't need that right now. I'll be at the backdoor."

"Are they coming over?" Eris asked when Rhea hung up the phone.

"Yeah. Rhode heard Artemis scream and shifted again, now he won't calm down," she explained as she came over to the bed and rested her hand on my shoulder, but her eyes never left Eris's.

"Ten thinks that being near her will calm him down?" Eris asked calmly.

"Or at least satisfy his need to protect her. I'm going to let them in, you settle her back down." Rhea gave my shoulder a firm squeeze before she left Eris to comfort me.

Once Eris was sure I had snapped out whatever had scared me so bad, she let me go. "Here," she reached over for the glass of water on the nightstand and offered it to me, "drink this."

I obeyed, taking long swallows of water until I couldn't drink anymore, the heaviness in my stomach calming me in some way. Eris took the glass and set it back on the nightstand before she helped me lay back down in the bed. "Can I have another blanket?" I was unable to keep my teeth from chattering or my body from quaking. "I'm cold."

"Sure." Eris smiled, taking another blanket that was folded at the end of the bed and settling it over me. She knelt next to me and took my hand in hers. "Jesus, you're like ice."

I closed my eyes, feeling all the drugs still coursing in my system and pulling me under as I fought the cold coursing through my veins. I groaned, fighting for consciousness at the sound of approaching feet and the clicking of something on the floor. I heard hushed voices and felt the bed sag beside me, but the warmth that came from whatever it was comforted me enough not to complain.

"I knew him," I mumbled sleepily, reaching out for the warmth that had come to comfort me and gripping it tightly.

"What did she say?" Rhea's voice asked urgently.

"It's okay," Eris whispered to me. "Just go to sleep, little bird. Everything's okay now."

"I knew him," I mumbled one last time before everything went dark, and I dropped off the face of the world.

Chapter 9

After everything that had happened in the past few days, I was more than grateful that for once I didn't dream, even if it was only for a couple of hours after I fell back to sleep. I didn't have to be calmed after screaming myself awake after a nightmare took hold; instead, this morning, for the first time in a long time, I was woken by a gentle touch to my head.

"Time to wake up, little bird," Eris's voice coaxed softly.

I made a small groan as I opened my eyes slowly to see Eris kneeling by my bedside, stroking my hair softly.

"Welcome back," she smiled when our eyes met, "you gave us quite a scare earlier."

"Shit," I groaned as everything flashed back to me. I sat up slowly and looked to the other side of the bed where I felt a familiar source of warmth from last night. Lying next to me, sleeping soundly, was Rhode's wolf.

"He heard you screaming last night," Eris explained. "He wouldn't calm down until he saw that you were safe, and then he wouldn't leave your side."

I looked at Eris then down at the wolf again, astonished by his protectiveness of me. I reached out and stroked his head. "I think I have a watchdog."

"It's not unheard of that spirit witches that can become connected to other witches," Eris remarked. "Instantly loyal, fiercely protective, willing to die for them. I guess Rhode being half shifter as well makes him twice as protective."

The wolf lifted his head then, looking up at me with those beautiful toffee eyes.

I scratched behind his ears. "Thank you for staying with me last night. I'm okay now, go see your brother."

The wolf didn't move right away, he just looked at me for another long moment as if he were trying to make sure I was really well enough for him to leave my side. I wondered how the wolf would know that, but I thought back to the kitchen when the wolf showed affection toward me when everyone feared he would show aggression. Rhode and I had connected on some level, whether we had known it or not, and that seemed to carry to his wolf in a more intense way.

Eris watched him go with a small smile on her face before turning her full attention back to me. "Are you okay?" Her blue eyes were soft and gentle, and I was grateful that I never saw any pity in them.

I shook my head, unsure exactly how to answer that. "I think so. I'm not really sure right now, everything's just really fuzzy." I ran a hand through my tangled hair that was still damp from my nightmare last night and still had twigs from the woods.

"Why don't you go take a shower and I'll make you breakfast?" Eris pulled a small leaf from my hair.

I nodded, the thought of a shower washing away all the craziness of last night more welcoming than anything at the moment.

It wasn't until I had stepped under the steaming water that I realized how cold I really was. I stood under the spray, just soaking in the warmth that I so desperately craved for some reason.

"Artemis," a dark whisper came from behind me.

I jumped at the sound, surprised that I wasn't alone "Eris?" I called out, thinking that she or Rhea had come to check on me. "Ray?"

When no answer came, I chalked it up to a crazy night and a splitting headache. I looked around, making sure I was alone in the bathroom before I went back to showering.

"Artemis," the whisper came again.

I nearly screamed this time, feeling as if whoever was there stood right behind me, breathing down my neck. I turned and saw no one, but I couldn't be crazy, I could feel someone watching me.

"We're coming for you, Artemis," the voice whispered again.

I covered my mouth in a desperate attempt not to start crying. "Go away." I closed my eyes as if I could shut it out. "Go away."

I cut my shower short, opting to freeze my ass off than have phantom whispers drive me crazy. I threw on a pair of jeans and a sweatshirt before I went down to the kitchen. I stopped just short as I heard everyone else in the kitchen, talking in hushed voices. I leaned against the wall and listened as they talked.

"I've never heard screams like that before," Rhode said. "Never. I didn't know that I had even shifted again into my wolf until he was howling."

"Are you sure this wasn't just a dream?" Tennessee asked.

I heard Rhea release a shaky sigh. "Who knows?"

"It wasn't just a dream, Ray," Eris said firmly. "Even when she had nightmares about Mom, she never screamed like that. What she felt was real."

There was a long stretch of silence before Rhea spoke again. "You think she had a vision?"

"I think that girl is coming into a magic that you and I can only imagine," Eris answered.

"If what you're saying is true, and that was a vision, then we are in a lot of trouble," Rhea said grimly.

I waited for a pause in the conversation before I made my entrance, hoping that no one would act weird or secretive around me now after everything that's happened.

Rhea was the first to notice me come in. "Hey. How are you feeling this morning?"

"I'm fine," I said quietly, making my way to the kitchen table where I damn near collapsed into my chair. I was still exhausted from the night before, and I had been too restless after my nightmare last night to get any real sleep. At this point I was pretty much running on fumes, but I refused to let anyone know that; the last thing they needed was another reason to worry about me.

The moment I sat down, Eris appeared with a small bowl of oatmeal with brown sugar, honey, and berries. Just like Mom used to make when I'd had a tough night. "Eat this," she said softly, "you need something in your stomach."

I just shook my head, feeling my stomach doing summersaults already. "I'm not hungry."

Rhea came over, placing her hand on my forehead, looking me over carefully as I prayed that she couldn't feel the chill on my skin. "Are you sure that you're okay to go to school?" she asked in a gentle voice that I didn't often hear from her. "You don't have to if you're not feeling up to it."

"It's high school, Ray, I think I can handle it."

"Okay." Rhea nodded, giving me one last once over before she was satisfied and ran her hand through my wet hair. "Then eat. I don't need you fainting at school."

I nodded and picked up my spoon, taking every bit of concentration I had to keep the spoon from shaking. I took a bite of oatmeal, but the second it hit my stomach, I felt the rising bile become too much to manage. I doubled over, puking my guts all over the floor.

"Shit," Rhea muttered, rushing over to my side and touching my face. "Artemis, honey, talk to me."

I didn't answer. I slumped over in my chair and was gone after that.

I came to in strong arms; someone had picked me up off the floor where I had fallen after passing out, so I gathered that I couldn't have been gone more than a few seconds, a minute tops.

"Take her upstairs," Rhea's voice said from far away.

"No," I said, not even sure if it was loud enough for anyone to hear.

"Are you back with us, little witch?" Tennessee asked, the closeness of his voice and the rumbling nearby letting me know he was the one that held me.

"Couch," was all I had the strength to say before I slumped into Tennessee's warm chest, fighting the urge to slip under again. I didn't want to be upstairs; the way I felt at this moment, I wouldn't have the stamina to make it down.

Tennessee obliged and carried me to the living room, settling me down on the couch. I felt a blanket drape over me and someone picked up my head and placed a pillow under it. I sagged completely, all my energy now gone—not that I had any to begin with since I hadn't even opened my eyes since I had come to.

"What is this?" Rhea asked in a hushed voice, but I could hear the worry that strained it.

"She just needs some rest," Tennessee said patiently. "She's been through a lot and she needs to regain her strength."

"Ray," Eris's voice said softly, "take Rhode to school and go to work. Tennessee and I will stay and watch Artemis."

I heard Rhea's voice catch and it felt like she was crying. I couldn't remember the last time I had seen Rhea cry. Had it been at Mom's funeral? I couldn't really remember anymore.

"Okay," she said, her voice barely a whisper. "Rhode, get your stuff. I'll be home as soon as I can, Eris."

"Don't worry, she's in good hands," Tennessee said. "Sleep, little witch, you need your rest."

I listened and, in the drop of a hat, fell away with the world.

Chapter 10

I came around to the sound of voices in the other room and the smell of something that made my mouth water. It took everything I had to open my eyes all the way and look around. I was still in the living room, lying on the couch, still groggy from the heavy sleep I had been in all morning.

I sat up slowly, taking nearly two entire minutes before I could get myself into a sitting position and stay there. I felt the sun streaming in through the windows and warming my skin, but it didn't seem to be enough. I pulled the blanket tighter around me as I tried to drive away the cold in my bones.

After allowing myself a moment to make sure everything was working together, I pushed myself off the couch and slowly walked into the kitchen. Eris was at the stove cooking, Tennessee watching her as she flew around the kitchen as she normally did. The look on his face wasn't just a look of boredom watching Eris, he had this look in his eyes that I only saw when I caught Rhode watching me when he thought I wasn't paying attention.

Tennessee's attention snapped to where I was the moment I stepped into the kitchen. He shot up from where he was sitting at a stool at the kitchen island and came over to me, helping me over to the kitchen table so I could sit down. I couldn't help but notice him watching me carefully as he did this, almost as if he thought I would faint again.

"Welcome back to the land of the living," he said evenly, sitting down next to me. "Did you have a good sleep?" A small smile came to his face.

I nodded, still trying to shake some of the haze off of me. "How long was I out?"

"You slept all morning, it's past noon."

"How many times did Ray call to check up on me?" My eyes locked onto Eris's.

"Twelve," she admitted with a soft sigh. She sighed as the phone on the counter started ringing. "Make that thirteen."

"I'm afraid that after the first couple of calls, I had to let Eris handle Rhea. She seems to be a little calmer in these situations." Tennessee smirked, his eyes going to Eris as she left the room, still trying to assure Rhea that I was okay.

"Eris has seen me at my very worst," I said. "I doubt anything would rattle her."

Tennessee's eyes cast downward to my right arm, where the tale tell scar told its story. "Is that your very worst?" he asked, reaching out slowly and running his thumb gently over the scar.

"Did Rhode tell you about it?"

Tennessee shook his head. "Do you want to tell me about it?"

"What's to tell? I was sad and fucked in the head. I made a bad decision." I left it at that.

"Alright," Eris said, bursting back into the kitchen at blinding speed, no longer on the phone. "Rhea's been quelled for now. So, let's have some lunch. Maybe if you can hold something down, Tennessee and I can answer the questions you have about what's going on."

I just nodded, my stomach still in knots; I wasn't hungry in the least, but I would grin and bear it if it meant that I could get the answers I desperately wanted.

I was able to hold down some lunch and, once Eris and Tennessee were convinced I was on the mend, we all sat in the living room. I stared down at my hands as Tennessee and Eris looked at me, waiting patiently for me to voice what was going on in my head.

"Take your time," Eris said softly, touching my hand.

"I honestly don't know where to start."

"Just ask whatever is on your mind," Tennessee said slowly.

"Tell me about the different types of witches," I said, looking to Tennessee.

"When a witch's magic comes into its own, it takes on an element, and in doing so that witch becomes in tune with that element. They can run in families like me and my brother, or they can all be different like you and your sisters."

"So, which one am I?"

"I don't know," he answered, "there are different affinities for different personality types. Water witches are very restless, they go wherever they feel the current sway."

"Just like Mom," I noted.

Tennessee nodded. "Your mother being a water witch would explain the constant traveling. Earth witches are strong willed and reliable, but can be very stubborn."

"That sounds like Ray," Eris said with a smirk on her face. "It also explains why she hated moving around so much, why she was so determined to settle and put down roots somewhere."

"Spirit witches are very intuitive and caring, they are also fiercely protective and very loyal," Tennessee continued. "Air witches are free spirits, they go with change well and they are ever the balance of harmony."

"That sounds like Eris," I said with a smile, remembering how she was always the buffer between Rhea and Mom when they butted heads, always trying to keep the peace between the two of them. "Tell me about fire witches."

"Fire witches are hot tempered but so very passionate. They aren't as rare as spirit witches but aren't as common as air, earth, or water witches, either." He paused for a moment and I saw something flash in his eyes. "Some witches think that fire witches are dangerous."

"Do you?" I wondered what my sisters would think of me if fire turned out to be the element my magic chose.

Tennessee smiled at me. "Of course not, little witch. It's just something that is heard now and again, there is no merit to it."

"Mom used to tell Rhea and me when we were girls that if she had to put money on it, you would be a fire witch," Eris said softly. "If that is what you turn out to be, then Rhea and I would be no less proud of you than we are now."

"Was Dad . . . ?" I started, falling off before I finished the question.

I had never met my father in person, I had only seen pictures that Mom had shown me growing up. The way the story went was that they fell in love after they met in Dublin, they got married and had Rhea, Eris, and I, but Dad decided that he didn't love Mom anymore and left us when I was just a baby. None of us had ever seen him since, and no one ever brought the subject of him up.

"No," Eris answered quietly. "Dad wasn't a witch."

"Did he know about Mom?"

She just shook her head. "If he did, then he didn't let on about it. Mom was pretty secretive about what she was."

"How am I supposed to know what to do? Is there like an instruction manual or is it like autopilot?"

"Once your magic starts to present itself, which we already suspect that it has," Tennessee explained, "then we'll begin teaching you the basics and, once we find out your affinity, then we can find someone of the same element to help you with that magic."

"So, there isn't like a witchy avatar state or anything?"

"You have got to stop watching so many cartoons," Eris sighed, "but yes. In times of extreme distress, some witches have been known to have gone into states like that."

"Once your magic starts to present itself, you'll develop what we call Gifts. I have a Gift for healing, Rhode a Gift for controlling and communicating with his wolf."

"What about you?" I asked Eris. "Do you and Ray have any Gifts?"

Eris nodded. "Rhea has a connection to the elements of nature around her and she can bend them to her will. Remember when she told you about what we were?"

I nodded a little, remembering Rhea making all those wildflowers spout and grow into full bloom just by willpower.

"I'm an empath," Eris continued. "I can sense what others are feeling and tune into it. It doesn't work 100% of the time, but I've managed to figure it out over the years."

At that moment, I suddenly understood Eris's constant fussing over me at over all these years; she could feel the swirl of emotions inside me, and it must have driven her crazy trying to help me through my emotional roller coaster this past year.

"I'm sorry, Eris," I whispered.

"Don't be sorry, little bird," she smiled. "I wouldn't be doing my job as your big sister if I didn't fuss over you all the time."

"Tell me about the Reapers," I said grimly.

"No one knows the original origin of Reapers," Tennessee explain evenly. "They're believed to have started back in Salem as fanatics of the church. Over the years, as people started to push witchcraft into fiction rather than reality, these fanatics were cast out by the church. Over time they've gone underground, teaching their beliefs to the next generation so that they might come about 'cleansing' the evil that they think witches bring. Reapers are determined in their mission and that makes them all the more dangerous to us."

"What does that mean for us now that they've made themselves known?" Eris asked.

"The same as it's always been," Tennessee answered. "We fight, we run if need be, and we survive."

"Ray said that my magic would present itself when it was time." I brought my eyes to look up at Eris. "What if it doesn't come in time to save me from the Reapers?"

Eris reached out and took my hand. "Magic or no, Rhea and I will protect you with everything we have, little sister. I won't let any harm come to you."

"As do I and my brother," Tennessee said softly, reaching over and taking my other hand and placing it over his heart. "You have my vow that I will protect you, little witch, with my life if it comes to it."

I nodded, a little numb from all this information. Rhode and Tennessee were the warriors that had come to protect me, but it was the ones that sought to destroy me that still frightened me. If what I saw last night—if it was even real—was any indication of what was to come then we were all in grave danger from these Reapers.

"THAT ONE LOOKS like a bunny," Eris said, pointing to the cloud that vaguely resembled a rabbit.

After I managed to stomach some lunch, Eris suggested we go outside and cloud watch like we used to when we were younger and bored out of our minds. I rested my head on the blanket laid out beneath us in the backyard.

"It only has one ear," I said.

"Rabbits can have one ear," she defended.

"When was the last time you saw a rabbit with one ear?"

"Just because you've never seen anything doesn't mean that it doesn't exist," she explained.

"That's actually exactly what that means," I said bluntly.

"Heads up," Tennessee called out the backdoor, "Rhea just pulled up."

I groaned a little at the statement; after being home all day with Eris and Tennessee, I didn't want to have to go through the process of convincing Rhea I was okay.

"It's okay," Eris said, standing up, her head blocking out the sun as she looked down at me. For a split second, she looked like an angel looking down on me. "I'll take the first wave, little bird, you just enjoy the sun."

"Always my advocate." I smiled softly.

"Until the day I die." She went back into the house.

I closed my eyes and stretched out, enjoying the warmth of the sun that had finally managed to chase away the chill that had been in my bones since last night. "I know you're out here Rhode," I said, opening one eye to see him standing a little off to the side from me. "The silent guy thing isn't really you're forte."

"You're feeling better?" He lied down beside me on the blanket.

"I am. I guess I just needed some R&R to let all the crap from last night get out of my system." I turned my head and looked at him for a moment. "I'm really sorry about being a brat last night."

"It's okay," he said, still looking up at the sky, "it's in the past."

"Then why are you acting so weird?" I asked. "You've barely said a word to me this morning and now you're all moody."

"You really want to know why?"

"Yes, I really want to know."

"I fucked up last night. I was assigned to watch you and protect you, and last night at that party, I just left you there. I abandoned you when I swore an oath to protect you with my life." He turned to look at me and I could see the shimmering of tears in those soft brown eyes. "I turned my back on you and you almost died. If something had happened to you, I would have never forgiven myself."

I looked at him for a second, stunned. I reached out and took his hand, interlacing our fingers together, and we both stared at the union for a moment. Rhode looked at me in surprise. "I know you're beating yourself up about this, but you came back for me. You came back for me and you called Ten and you got me home safe and sound. You may think you've failed in your duty, but I think you did just that. You protected me."

Rhode rolled his head away from me in an effort to try and hide his tears, but I could see his shoulders shake hard as he cried silently. I didn't say anything to try and console him or calm him, I just sat there and held his hand as long as he let me.

"Artemis," Rhea called from the backdoor. "Can you and Rhode come into the kitchen for a moment?"

"Yeah," I replied without moving from where I was, "give us a sec." I looked over at Rhode, who had gone very still and was back to looking at the sky. "Are you ready to go back inside?"

"Yeah," he said in a small rasp of a voice.

"Hey," I whispered, rolling over to my side and touching the side of Rhode's face gently. My sapphire blues met those beautiful toffee browns of his and I traced his jawline with my fingertips. "Don't you ever think less of yourself. You are my protector, and never for a moment will I ever doubt that."

When we came into the kitchen, Eris, Rhea, and Tennessee were all sitting at the table. They all looked up at me and Rhode as we came in. Rhode sat next to Tennessee while I sat between Eris and Rhea.

"Are you feeling better?" Rhea asked softly, placing a hand to my cheek.

"I'm fine," I assured her. "What's going on?"

"We need to finish the discussion we were having this morning." She refused to bring up my illness that forced the discussion to a halt.

"I went back to the woods last night to look for the Reapers that Artemis stabbed," Ten said evenly.

I saw something pass over his face and my stomach dropped. I felt like I was going to be sick again. "You didn't find him, did you?"

Tennessee hesitated and all but confirmed my fears before he even opened his mouth. "No, I didn't."

"Artemis," Eris said quietly, turning to me, "last night, when you had your nightmare . . . you said you knew him. What did you mean by that?"

"The Reaper in my dream, I felt like I knew him. His eyes, they were blue. Blue like mine . . . like Mom's." The room fell deadly quiet after what

I said. "Why do I feel like you all know something I don't?" Everyone at the table exchanged knowing glances.

"Honey, I think you had a vision last night. It wasn't just a nightmare," Eris said.

"Why now?" I asked, stunned. "I thought I didn't have any magic yet."

"There isn't a set formula for how this is supposed to work," Rhea explained. "Your Gift could have been triggered by any number of things; it could have been brought on by the drugs or the alcohol or just the attack by the Reapers."

"Do these visions always come true?" The memory of that Reaper killing that young boy in my dream made me shiver.

"I don't know." Rhea's voice was pained that she couldn't ease my fears of what I had seen.

I cleared my throat. "What does this mean now?

"It means that we establish some ground rules," Rhea said firmly. "First of which is that you are never alone. When you're at school you're with Rhode, and if you're out of this house you're with one of us."

"Okay." I nodded. "I can handle that."

"Second, no lying. If you sense in the slightest something is wrong, you tell one of us."

"Okay."

"The last one is the most important," she said in a low voice. "If you see Reapers again, then you run. You find Rhode or Ten and you leave New Orleans. With or without us."

I looked to Eris who was looking just as serious as Rhea. "Eris?" I hoped she would say something, anything to the contrary. She said nothing, only wiped a small tear from her cheek.

"You go to Izzy's in the mountains and you hide. You don't come back, not for anything. Am I understood?" Rhea continued.

"Ray." I breathed, shaking my head, but her eyes were dead set on what she had just told me.

"Am I understood?" Rhea asked again, firmly. "You are destined to be a powerful witch, Artemis, and I won't let anything happen to you."

"Stop it!" I stood up from the table as I tried hard to hold on to what little control I had. "I'm so sick of everyone thinking that I am this great and powerful witch. I'm not what everyone thinks I am."

Rhea took my hands in hers, gently pulling me back down into my seat. I looked over at her, tears spilling down my face as a hundred different emotions coursed through me. "Your magic will make itself known when it's time and not before, Artemis. I've believed that you are going to be powerful from the moment I first saw you when you were born, and I am not wrong in believing that. You are destined for greatness, and my job as your big sister is to make sure that you're in this world long enough to achieve . . . even if that means giving up my life for yours."

I turned away from her, wiping the tears from my eyes, embarrassed that everyone's seeing all these emotions come out now. "I'm sorry," I said, "first Mom, now all this? It's a lot to process, a lot, and I'm afraid that I haven't been processing it very well."

"You're doing just fine, little bird," Rhea said, placing her index finger under my chin and turning my head so that I could face her. "I know it's a lot, but all of us are here to help you through it. I need you to truly believe that."

"I do." I nodded.

"Good. Are you okay?" she asked.

"Yeah, Ray, I'm fine."

Rhea looked over to Eris as if she needed confirmation that of what I was telling her. "Is she?"

"She's keeping down solid food and she has more energy. She's fine, Rhea."

"Good." Rhea nodded. "For now, you go back to school and we act like everything is normal. Okay?"

I nodded. I could play the normal card for now; hell, I'd been playing that years before any of this happened. Somehow the weirdest people were the ones that tried to act the most like they were normal.

Chapter 11

"Y ou are going down!" I taunted.

"In your dreams," Rhode countered.

We were over at his place playing *Call of Duty*, Eris and Rhea both had a shift at the store and, after over an hour of begging, they had allowed me to spend the day at Rhode and Tennessee's house.

Tennessee had his own rules as well: Rhode and I had to be in his sight and in a common area, and we were definitely not allowed to be alone together. Despite the argument from both Rhode and I that we weren't going to do anything of the sort, Tennessee refused to back down.

Hence the playing of violent video games in Rhode's living room with his older brother staring at us from the kitchen. Rhode and I had been playing for a couple of hours and I was kicking his butt good.

"How are you so good at this?" Rhode asked cautiously as I launched a grenade at his character and flew him to bits.

"I was basically a shut-in for a year," I said evenly. "Rhea's boyfriend, Mattie, used to come over a lot. Instead of making me talk to him and carry on a conversation like everyone else was, we'd just sit there and play videogames, he'd bring over a new one every week and we'd just sit there in silence for hours while we played. It was really nice, actually."

"Whatever happened to Mattie?"

I shrugged. "He stopped coming around, but he left me his Xbox and I still play from time to time, but it's not as much fun by myself."

"You are entirely something else," Rhode said softly.

"You are road kill!" I smiled, jumping up off the couch in victory. I winced as a twinge of pain shot through my back when I stood up, but I did my best to play it off so that Rhode wouldn't notice.

The thing was, Tennessee did notice.

"Rhode, go take the trash out," he said, standing up from the kitchen table and coming into the living room.

"Seriously? Right now?" Rhode asked, his tone deflated.

"Go, little brother, before I make you do laps around the neighborhood."

Rhode did as he was told, but I could see the look of absolute teenage defiance all over his face. As soon as Tennessee and I were alone, he motioned for me to sit on the couch. I sat down but I could feel my back spasm and I had to lie down to try and make the pain stop.

"Why didn't you tell anyone you were hurt?" Tennessee asked in a soft voice, rolling me over so that I was on my stomach. He gently ran his hand over my back through my shirt until he found the spot where the pain was unbearable.

"It didn't start bothering me until this morning," I answered. "Must have been from when the Reaper slammed me into the tree."

There was a small tension from Tennessee at what I had said. "Is it okay if I lift up your shirt and look?"

I nodded. "You have my permission."

Tennessee moved slowly with precise and deliberate motions, I could feel the air hit my naked back as Tennessee examined me. "It's bruised rather badly," he said, pulling my shirt back down. "I can heal it for you if you like. If not, I can give you an ice pack and something for the pain."

"You can heal me," I said, unable to keep the smile off my face at how polite he was with me; he had never so much as raised his voice to me since I had met him.

I could feel one of Tennessee's hands on my lower back and the other in the spot between my shoulder blades. Almost immediately I felt a beautiful and radiating warmth spread through my back, better than any heating pad.

After a minute of two, the warmth faded and I lay there on the couch, still in the afterglow of the healing. "I thought you were an asshole," I confessed, still a little dazed.

"Did you?" Tennessee asked curiously.

"I hadn't really met you yet," I clarified. "I only saw you when you were mad at Rhode, and you looked really mean then."

"I can see why you made those assumptions. I'm hard on my brother because I care about him. Rhode knows that, and I think that he resents me a little for it."

"Yes, I know the feeling."

"Were you really mad about Rhode spending the night at my place?" I asked. "Or when we took your car and went to the French Quarter?"

"Not mad, I just wanted to make sure that Rhode was thinking with his head when it came to you. We're here for a reason, and you come before anything else to us."

"Yeah, because Rhode's not here to get his dick wet," I said, a little bitter at that.

"I'm sorry you heard that, I didn't mean any offense by it. I see now that Rhode really does care about you, and that his mission is to protect you." Tennessee rested his hand on my head and whispered softly, "Get some sleep, little witch. Let your back recover."

I nodded, my eyes already getting heavy now that Tennessee had suggested the thought. I closed my eyes, hearing the distant sound of the door opening.

"What's going on?" Rhode asked.

"She's going to sleep for a bit," Tennessee said softly. "You and I, little brother, are going to spar in the backyard."

I heard their footsteps fade as they walked away from me and I faded away from the world.

When I woke my back felt a lot better. The place was still quiet but I heard muffled sounds coming from outside. I got off the couch and went to investigate, seeing through the sliding glass backdoor that Tennessee and Rhode were outside fighting. It didn't look like they were trying to hurt each other, but they were really going at it and looked like they had been for a while.

I opened the door and came out quietly, sitting on the porch and watching them. Rhode was strong and fast, but Tennessee seemed to have more control over his strength, so he let Rhode tire himself out before he got him right where he wanted him. Tennessee pinned Rhode to the ground and I knew he had the drop.

"Nice try, little brother." Tennessee grinned at Rhode before getting off of him. He offered him a hand and helped him up off the ground. "You know you'll never be able to beat me."

"One of these days, old man," Rhode teased.

Tennessee wrapped his arm around Rhode's neck and pulled him in, kissing the top of his head. "In your dreams."

I watched the two of them as they walked back toward the house, still in their own little world until they both noticed me as I sat quietly. "Hey," Rhode said breathlessly, sitting next to me on the porch. "How'd you sleep?"

"No dreams," I said softly. I had only been sleeping for an hour at the most, but it still felt nice not to have nightmares invade my sleep.

"How's the back?" Tennessee asked, ignoring Rhode's confused face at the question.

"Better, thank you."

Tennessee conceded a small smile and nodded toward me. "I'll go make us some lunch. Can you two manage to keep your hands off each other while I do that?"

"Seriously?" Rhode asked. "It stopped being funny like three hours ago."

I could see the pleasure on Tennessee's face at still being able to rag on his baby brother, before he walked past us and went into the house. I leaned into Rhode and rested my head against his shoulder, not caring that he was sweaty.

"Your brother really loves you," I said softly as we stared out at nothing in particular.

"He does," Rhode affirmed, "and I love him, too. He's my teacher, my parent, and my best friend." I felt him pause for a moment as if he were thinking. "One of my best friends."

His amendment made me smile; even with everything falling out of sorts just when I thought I had gotten everything in my life back together, things were starting to even out again, and I knew deep down that Rhode had something to do with it. I did know one thing for sure.

I definitely owed Rhode $20.

Chapter 12

"**D**id you sleep alright?" Eris asked when I came down into the kitchen Monday morning.

"No nightmares," was my answer as I sat down at the table. It was true, despite my restful weekend, I had slept so fitfully last night that I hadn't gotten a deep enough sleep to dream. Aside from me nearly dead on my feet from lack of sleep I was fine, and I didn't want to stay home another day from school only to have my sisters worry about something they had no power over. "Coffee?"

"If you eat something, I don't want only coffee in your stomach," Eris bargained. "A waffle and some bacon."

"Pop-Tart," I countered.

"Fine," she caved, handing me a package of strawberry Pop-Tarts and placing a cup of coffee in front of me. "Eat both of them."

"Aye, aye captain." I opened the package and put one in my mouth.

I looked over at the tapping at the backdoor and smiled when I saw Rhode standing there in his jeans and a flannel shirt. I couldn't hide the smile from Eris as she went to answer the door. "Good morning, Rhode," she greeted. "Breakfast?"

He shook his head as he came inside and sat next to me. "Nah, but thanks."

I offered him my other Pop-Tart and he took it, placing it in his mouth and allowing it to hang out rather than taking a bite. "Did I miss anything good at school on Friday?" I asked.

Rhode took a bite out of the Pop-Tart and shook his head, reaching around me to snag my cup of coffee, taking a sip from the cup. "Nothing to write home about. Caleb was looking for you, though."

"Was he?" I asked coyly. With everything that had happened since the first day of school, I hadn't even had time to remember that I might have liked Caleb. Even if I did, did I like him as much I liked Rhode? Did I even like Rhode the way he liked me? It was all too much to sort out at this time. "What did you say to him?"

"Told him that I hadn't seen you since I took off at the party."

"Did he believe you?" I reached over to take a sip of coffee from my cup before setting it in front of Rhode, allowing him to finish the rest.

"He seemed to. I don't think that he had any reason not to."

"Good." I nodded.

"What are you going to do when you see him?" Rhode asked, clearly seeing the confusion on my face.

I shook my head, having no clue what of that. "Let's burn that bridge when we get to it."

"Good deal," he said. "You grab your stuff and I'll meet you outside. Do you want to walk or drive?"

"Walk." I was in the mood for a good conversation this morning and hoped that the walk to school would do me some good.

Rhode kissed the top of my head before he finished off the cup of coffee and headed out the door. It wasn't until Rhode had left that I was completely aware of Eris leaning against the sink, watching everything that had gone one between us.

"So," she started with a cat-that-ate-the-canary grin on her face, "you and the cute neighbor boy have been spending quite a bit of time together?"

"Rhode and I are friends; in fact, he's my only friend at the moment, so yeah, we're going to spend a lot of time together."

"I'm your big sister, Artemis, and I know that look on your face when you see Rhode. That is a more-than-friendship look."

"Can we deal with the homicidal pack of Reapers that are trying to kill me first? If we manage to square that away then you can harass me about my love life."

"Deal," Eris said, placing a canvas bag in front of me. "Make sure you eat, even if you're not hungry. If you feel faint, text Rhode and he'll get to you."

"Yes Mom," I said slowly, taking the bag off the counter.

"I love you, little bird." She smiled softly. "Have a good day at school."

"CAN I ASK you a question?" I asked Rhode as we walked to school, me taking my sweet time as I honestly had no desire to go back to school but every desire to get out of that house.

"I've asked you quite a few, so it seems fair," he answered casually, keeping up with my leisurely pace.

"What happened to your dad?" I noticed the hesitation in his next step, and I felt completely embarrassed that I had even touched the subject. Some people didn't like to bring up their daddy issues, and seeing as I didn't really even have a dad to speak of, I should have known better. "Sorry, I shouldn't have asked."

"You show me your scars and I'll show you mine," Rhode said with a dark smile.

"Nothing to tell, really, my dad split when I was a baby. Never met the man and I probably never will," I said. "Your father was a Shifter?"

Rhode nodded. "Shifters marrying outside their own kind isn't very common, mostly because it's almost impossible to have children unless it's with another Shifter. Ten thinks because my parents' love was so strong and my mother's magic was so powerful, it allowed them to be the exception to the rule."

"So, what happened to him?" I asked carefully.

"My dad was killed by Reapers when I was three," he said evenly. "A couple of Reapers broke into our house one night. Dad told us to run while he fended them off. Said he would be right behind us." Rhode fell off as if he had lost himself in the memory. "I don't really remember him that well."

"Parents lie to us sometimes," I said softly, remember Mom telling me the same thing before I never saw her again. "Whether they truly believe that lie or if they're just protecting us, they lie."

"Jesus, we're fucked up." Rhode chuckled as we reached the school.

"Yeah, we are," I agreed. I paused as we passed a long row of flyers posted along the walls. They were missing person's flyers, and I knew the guy on them. He was the guy I had seen killed by the Reapers the night of the party.

"What's wrong?" Rhode asked when he noticed my fixation on the flyers.

"Who is this guy?" I asked quietly, unable to take my eyes off of the picture.

"That's Danny," Rhode said, thrown by my interest in this guy. "He's some sophomore that sits behind me in Spanish. I think I might've seen him at the party. Why are you asking me this?"

I just shook my head, hoping that all of this was in my head. "No reason. I'll see you at lunch?" I stopped at my locker to pick up my books for the first couple of periods.

"Where else would I be?" Rhode smiled, winking at me before he kept walking down the hall toward his first class. "Text me if you need anything."

I gave him a little salute and slammed the door to my locker, nearly jumping out of my skin when Caleb leaned against the locker next to mine, looking at me with a wolfish grin.

"Christ!" I gasped.

My surprise only made his smile wider. "How are you today, gorgeous? I missed you on Friday."

"Yeah, sorry, my hangover was of epic proportions. Whatever that shit was that you gave me, I was obliterated."

"Best high of your life though, right?"

"That it was," I noted grimly.

"Well, if you're in the mood to get obliterated again tonight, I think I might be able to help you with that."

I opened my mouth to say something but faltered when I looked at Caleb. I didn't know exactly what it was, but there was a shadow that crossed his face that made my body shiver and my blood run cold. "I actually can't," I said, hoping that I had made a graceful recovery in the conversation. "My sisters found out and, needless to say, I'm grounded."

"How long?"

"I believe the words 'college graduation' were used."

"So, sneak off again. What's the worst that could happen?"

"Oh, you really don't know my sisters that well," I quipped. "Look, I'd rather not double down on the amount of trouble that I'm already in, but thanks."

Caleb looked at me for a long time and I did my best not to squirm under his gaze until he was satisfied with what I was saying. "Okay."

"Have you heard about this Danny kid that went missing?" I asked, trying to change the subject. "Have you ever met this kid?"

Caleb shook his head. "I've sold to the guy a couple of times, but all I heard was that he disappeared after the party and his parents haven't heard from him since. Heard he got in with some bad people."

"What do you think happened to him?" My heart raced as flashes of my dream came back to me, seeing Danny's face as the life left his eyes.

"Who knows," Caleb shrugged, "but if the rumors are true, they won't find his body."

"What do you mean by that?"

"Around here, when criminals kill someone, they dump their body in the bayou. Let the alligators get him. No body, no evidence." Caleb's lips curled into a dark smile that shook me to my core.

"Jesus, that's dark," I whispered.

"Don't worry, I'm sure the kid's just sleeping off a bender and he'll turn up in a couple of days," Caleb offered, but the dark shadow that surrounded him didn't alleviate my anxiety. "Give me a call when you get out of jail."

He gave me one last glance over his shoulder before he headed down the hallway.

That look nearly made my heart stop beating.

———◆❋◆———

"ARE YOU OKAY?" Rhode's voice snapped me out of the trance I seemed to be in since I had my run in with Caleb this morning.

"Yeah, I'm fine," I answered, almost a little too quickly. Rhode's eyes fell to my hands, which were twitching badly on the table. I pulled them back and shoved them in my lap, but he had already seen the damage.

"We said no lying, remember?" He reached over and took my hands into his. "What's wrong?"

"You remember the night after the party? When I had that dream?" Rhode nodded.

"I saw Danny in my dream. He got murdered by a Reaper in front of my eyes. They used him to get information about me and my sisters and, once they didn't need him anymore, they killed him."

"It's okay," Rhode said softly.

"No, it's not," I choked out. "I think that Caleb is involved with these Reapers and I think that he may have had a hand in killing Danny. I saw this shadow around him . . ." I fell off as remembering what it was that made me shiver. "I don't want to be around him, Rhode. Not today, not ever again."

"I'm not going to let him anywhere near you," Rhode said in a low voice as he squeezed my hands. "I promise you that."

"Thank you," I whispered.

"What's this?" Rhode asked, looking at the face I had drawn in my notebook during class. I had never been an artist, I couldn't even fake being one, but this drawing was a detailed human face. The only problem was that I didn't know who this person was as I had never seen him before in my life.

"I don't know, but this is the one from my vision. The one that killed Danny."

"The one you saw that night in the woods?"

"Yeah, only I don't think that it was a vision," I realized out loud. "He could see me and he could talk to me. I don't know what it was, but he saw me."

Rhode looked at me and then at the drawing. "How do you know what his face looks like if you've never seen him without his mask?

I looked at Rhode and I knew that he could see the fear that was on my face. "I have no idea."

Our conversation was interrupted by the bottle blonde from the archery field who came up to our table like she was hot shit and I was to stop everything I was doing just to accommodate her.

Fuck that shit.

"Can I help you?"

She leaned over the table and got so close I could see the colored contacts that confirmed he eyes were not in fact baby blue, but in fact, a dull and muddy brown. "Stay away from Caleb," she seethed, "he's mine."

"You can have him sweetie, I'm not interested."

"I know all about you," she hissed.

"Do tell," I said coolly, wondering what the gossip mill had spread about me in the first three days of school. I might have been the only person crazy enough to want to hear the rumors about myself.

"Not a good idea," Rhode warned her in a calm voice.

"I know that you're some catatonic bitch who couldn't function after your drunk of a mother drove her car off a bridge," she hissed, leaning in and getting close to my face.

That was all she managed to get out before I leapt across the table and tackled her to the floor. The entire dining hall erupted in cheers and shouts as we wrestled around on the floor. I soon gained the upper hand and was bashing the bottle blonde's head against the floor when Rhode pulled me off of her. I kicked against him, wanted to keeping bashing that fucking twat's head against the floor.

"That's enough darlin'," he breathed in my ear in a firm voice. "She's down. It's over."

It took every ounce of self-control I had to stop myself from trying to break free of his grip. I calmed myself and, after Rhode was sure I wouldn't try to make a break for it, his grip around me loosened.

"Are we good?" His eyes leveled mine as the entire cafeteria stared at us.

I nodded, unable to get my state of mind together enough to speak.

The entire cafeteria fell silent as the principal came in and surveyed the scene before pointing directly at me and signaling for me to follow him. Rhode took my hand in his as he walked with me out of the cafeteria.

———◆◆◆———

"You did that on purpose, didn't you?"

I opened my eyes and looked over at Rhode. We sat outside the principal's office while Rhea and Eris were in the office hashing out my punishment for assaulting the school's star pupil. "Beat up that stuck-up, bottle-blonde bitch?" I said with a small smile of satisfaction. "Yeah, I did."

"You could have dropped her in one blow. We both know that," Rhode said, ignoring my misdirect and trying to get to the root of the problem. "You wanted to fight her and you wanted to make a spectacle of it."

I didn't answer him, closing my eyes and rolling my head back to face up against the ceiling.

"Is this about Caleb?" Rhode probed. "Do you want to be away from him that badly?"

I opened my eyes and sat up straight in my chair, looking Rhode dead in the eyes as I spoke quietly. "If you could have felt what I did around him today . . . It felt dark and wrong. Caleb was involved in Danny's murder, and whatever else is going on, it's bad, Rhode.

"Artemis," Rhode breathed, but he stopped when the door to the principal's office opened. Eris came out of the principal's office followed by Rhea, who looked beyond pissed.

"Well, you're suspended," Eris said in a casual voice. It wasn't my first time at the rodeo in this department.

"You're lucky you're only suspended and not expelled," Rhea seethed, not even bothering to break her stride as she kept walking down the hall.

"Pity," I said as Rhode and I stood and followed my sisters out of the school. "Would have been my personal best getting bounced after a week."

Rhea didn't say a thing on the way home. No, she saved up all that anger until we got back, because the minute she closed that door behind us, she laid into me like she never had before.

"What were you thinking?" she asked. I could tell she wanted to scream it at me, but God forbid we got the neighbor's attention.

I sat on the couch and looked up at Rhea, trying to ensure that one of us kept our cool in this conversation. "I needed to get out of school, away from those people."

"Why didn't you call Eris or me? Taking you out for being sick would have been easier than started a fight."

"Not nearly as much fun, though," I quipped.

"Do you think that this is a joke, Artemis?"

"I, uh . . ." My words fell off as the most intense pain ripped through my skull, damn near blinding me. I put my hand to my head as if that would alleviate some of the pressure, but the pain only continued to build and intensify.

"Artemis, what is it?" Rhea asked.

I didn't answer her, or maybe I couldn't, or maybe the two were interchangeable at the moment, but all I could manage was concentrating on my breathing.

"She's having a vision," I heard Eris's voice say from I don't know where.

I felt a hand on my knee and Rhea say, "Artemis, what do you see?"

Only I was too far gone to answer her.

"Artemis!" Rhea cried.

Then the world went black.

I was standing in the corner of a hospital room and I could hear a woman screaming. I looked around, seeing the ugly mint-green painted hospital walls and the white, black, and mint-green linoleum floor tiles.

I stepped forward and saw the screaming coming from a woman in a hospital bed, her legs up in stirrups as a doctor kneeled at her feet.

Shit, she was giving birth.

"I need you to push," the doctor said, the woman giving another big scream.

As I kept walking forward I took her sweat-drenched blonde hair, so blonde that it resembled a halo around her head. She looked up as the doctor told her to push again and I could see a set of beautiful sapphire-blue eyes.

"Mom?" I said numbly, but no one answered me.

"Congratulations, it's a baby girl," the doctor announced.

Mom fell back against the bed, smiling as the doctor handed the baby to the nurse. "Artemis," she said softly as she held the little bundle close to her chest. "I had a dream about you, my little bird."

The nurse came over and collected the baby from my mother's arms, taking her away and cleaning her up before wrapping the baby up in a little pink blanket and a little pink beanie on her head.

Mom watched from the bed, a small smile on her face as she watched the nurse place her newborn child into a basinet.

Only, the look of peace on her face didn't last long as I saw it fall and her joy turn into screams of pain.

"Hold on," the doctor said, moving back into the catching position. "It looks like we've got another one here."

Another one? I thought as I watched Mom go through the process of delivering another baby, but this wasn't the same as the last time. I could see worry and terror on my mother's face as the doctor coached her through pushing all over again.

I came closer to her and heard her praying under her breath, but it wasn't in English and I didn't understand what she was saying or who she was saying it to.

"Congratulations, this one's a boy," the doctor said, wrapping the newborn in a blanket and resting him on my mother's stomach as a nurse cut the umbilical cord.

"Apollo." Mom smiled, but it wasn't the joyous smile she had given me, it was a sad smile. Almost heartbroken. "My little prince, I dreamed this day would come and I'm still not ready for how beautiful you are, my precious baby boy."

The nurse smiled at my mother as she took the baby boy away to clean him, handing him off in exchange for the baby girl bundled in a pink blanket that was supposedly me. The doctor handed me over to Mom. I saw her sadness fade away, replaced by something hopeful.

She held me close as the nurse and the doctor filed out of the room, leaving her alone. She looked up and, for a moment, I thought that she could actually see me. "I am begging you not to do this, John. This doesn't have to happen."

I turned to see who she was talking to. Behind me I saw a man standing against the wall, holding the baby boy who was now bundled with a blue blanket. "Don't," he said in a clipped voice. "You have fulfilled your duty to me, and now I have no more use for you."

"These are children, for God's sake," Mom snapped back. "These are our children and you want to pit your daughter against your son. You want your children to kill each other, and for what?"

"Don't lecture me about this."

"What about our other children? What am I going to tell Rhea and Eris when I come home and their father is gone?"

The man said nothing, looking down at the little blue bundle with no emotion or curiosity on his face.

"You have your son, and I hope to God that you don't raise him with the hate that you harbor in your heart, John. Now go, and don't you ever darken our door again."

He said nothing, but I saw his short black hair and his cold green eyes look to my mother before he left the room with the baby.

Madame Josephine's words echoed through my head as I watched the scene unfold before me. *There is an older man, a man from your past, who will try to destroy you. He will wield a weapon in the form of a young warrior, another man from your past.*

"Dad?" I breathed, feeling myself plummet out.

I gasped for air as if I had been holding my breath under water for decades. I looked around and saw myself back in the real world, back in my living room in New Orleans. I noticed somewhere between getting home and waking up that I had been moved from the couch to the floor. My head was resting in Eris's lap with Rhea and Tennessee at my sides, looking down at me with worried eyes.

"Artemis?" Rhea's voice swam through the layers of cotton wrapped around my brain as I just stared up at her. She reached out and touched my face, and it felt as if I were struck by lightning, my body twisting off the ground from the shock of the contact.

"Apollo," the words came from my lips before my mind even registered that I could speak. I had no conscious meaning of what that word meant, but the thought of it sent shivers through my body and made my veins turn ice cold.

"What did she say?" Rhea's voice was deadly and urgent as her eyes locked onto Eris's, something unspoken passing between the two of them.

"Apollo," I breathed again, this time truly afraid of that name.

Then the world went black.

Chapter 13

"Artemis!" *Eris's voice came in a worried cry.*

"She's seizing," Tennessee said in an urgent tone. "Roll her onto her side."

"You're going to be okay, little bird," Rhea said softly.

I awoke with a sharp gasp, closing my eyes against the flood of information my brain wasn't ready to receive. I don't know where I went when the world went black, it was a place that dreams and lights didn't seem to reach. When I came back everything seemed foreign for a minute, like things weren't quite right, until my brain registered that I was in my bed.

I opened my eyes again, slowly, allowing my senses to readjust. I was unsurprised to find Rhode sat in a chair that had been pulled up next to my bed, worry in those warm eyes of his. He was leaning forward and his hands were pressed together and I couldn't tell for sure, but it looked like he was praying.

"Hey," he said softly once our eyes met.

I wanted to sit up, but I didn't have the strength to command it of myself. "What happened?"

"You don't remember?" Rhode asked with a small frown.

He reached out and stroked my hair as I tried to use all of my concentration to recall what happened after we got home. "I remember us getting home and Ray reading me the riot act, then there was this pain in my head and I blacked out."

"Your sisters think that you had a vision," Rhode filled in for me. "You were gone almost twenty minutes before you came back."

I looked at him and saw something pass behind his eyes. "What happened after I came back?"

"You said something, a name," he said, hesitating slightly, "then you had a seizure."

"A seizure?"

Rhode nodded. "Lasted almost two minutes." He reached out and took my hand between both of his, bring it to his lips and kissing it. "Scariest two minutes of my life."

"How long have I been out?" I asked, unable to account for the time I had lost, or even guess at that point.

"A few hours," he said, "it's a little after midnight."

"So, the wolf didn't come out this time?" I reached out my hand to cover the small distance between our bodies and touched his chest just above where his heart was.

"No." Rhode shook his head, placing his hand over mine. "Took more self-control than I've ever had to use before, but I was able to keep him in." Rhode smiled for a second before it vanished and the intimate moment we had been sharing went with it. "What did you see, Artemis? What did you see that made you look so afraid?"

I didn't answer his question, not because I wouldn't but because something deep inside of me was legitimately terrified by what I saw. "What did I say when I came back?" I asked. "Before I had the seizure?"

Rhode tensed visible before he forced himself to relax. "You said a name. Apollo. Who is that, Artemis?"

I summoned all my strength to sit up on the bed; it wasn't enough and Rhode had to help me all the way up. "Where is everyone?"

"Ten is downstairs in the kitchen with your sisters, trying to sort out what happened."

"Okay." I nodded.

I managed to get out of bed on my own, but I did need Rhode's help to get down the stairs. After I managed to get to the bottom floor, I chose to brace myself against the wall and walk on my own. I could tell that Rhode objected and wanted to help, but it was my own damn pride that didn't want it.

I paused just outside the kitchen as I heard the voices of Tennessee and my sisters speaking and, as usual these past few days, the subject was me. I leaned against the wall, wanting to hear what they had to say about what happened when I wasn't in the room. I looked at Rhode who shook his head, but my only response was to raise a single finger to my lips to tell him to be quiet. He didn't agree with me, but he didn't make a sound as we listened.

"She said his name," Rhea said, her voice strained as she said it.

"That can't be possible," Eris said, her voice just as edgy as Rhea's.

"Why?" Tennessee was the odd man out in this one, and I knew he was confused.

I stood in the doorway of the kitchen now, but no one's attention was brought to me until I spoke. "We're not supposed to be able to see the past," I said softly. "No witch ever has. Visions have only been of the future. Isn't that right, Ray?"

Rhea nodded as I came into the kitchen with Rhode not too far behind me and sat down at the table next to Eris, Rhode taking a seat between myself and Tennessee. "No witch has ever claimed to have seen visions of the past, so this is a first for us, yes."

"Welcome back, little witch," Tennessee said softly through the tense air in the room. "How do you feel?"

"Better," I said quietly, waiting for the shoe to drop. Whatever I had said when I had come back from my vision had something to do with whatever the Reapers were doing and why they were after me. Rhea and Eris had been terrified by what I had said, and I knew there was going to be a long conversation behind it as the pieces of the puzzle started to come together in my head.

"Do you want something to eat?" Eris asked, clearly anxious now. "You slept through dinner."

I shook my head. "I'm fine."

"So, what does this mean?" Tennessee asked, discarding the pleasantries and getting back to the important matter at hand. "That Artemis can see the past?"

"The only witches I know that I have ever seen the past are Watchers," Rhea said.

"A Watcher?" Tennessee asked. "There hasn't been a Watcher in generations, they're rare enough as it is, almost wiped from the earth. You think that Artemis has that Gift?"

"What's a Watcher?" I asked.

"There have been witches that can have visions of the future," Eris explained quietly. "Our bloodlines have witches that have had visions, myself included, but Watchers can see all. Past, present and future. It's all one fluid stream to them."

"So why am I getting the feeling that there's something the two of you aren't telling me?" Tennessee said slowly, his eyes locked dead onto Rhea, who refused to make eye contract. "Why did Artemis call out that name? Who is Apollo?"

"Our baby brother," I answered for her, all eyes shifted to me once I said it. "My twin."

"There's no record of your mother giving birth to a boy," Tennessee said in a quiet voice, taking in this new piece of information.

"That's because he was stillborn," Rhea said darkly, her eyes sliding to mine. "At least, that's what Mom told us."

"Only he didn't die," I breathed, the memory of that little baby boy coming back to me.

"What do you mean?" Eris asked.

"In my vision, I saw him being born. I saw him take breath and live."

"Jesus," Eris gasped, covering her mouth with both of her hands.

"What else did you see?" Rhea asked, her voice dark and shaking.

"She gave him to a man, and that man left with him," I explained, remembering that man with the black hair and fierce green eyes.

"Do you remember what he looked like?" Rhea asked.

I hesitated for a moment before I said in a hushed voice, "I think it was Dad."

Rhea eyes widen as she looked at me. "Are you sure?"

I nodded. "He looked just like he did in the photo Mom showed me. The one with you and Eris right before Mom got pregnant with me."

Rhea got up from her seat and paced the length of the kitchen, her face pale and worried. "Goddamn it," she swore.

"What does this mean, Ray?" I asked. "What happens now?"

Rhea stopped pacing and looked at me. "We need to meet with the Elders immediately."

Chapter 14

Since we couldn't just take off in the middle of the night, Tennessee and Rhode slept over at our place and, at the crack of dawn, Rhea had us pulling out and driving to the French Quarter to the rather large compound where the Elder's resided.

We were met at the door by a young blonde girl who had to be all of fourteen. She took Eris, Rhea, and Tennessee to meet someone, leaving Rhode and I in the middle of a covered courtyard twiddling out thumbs as we waited for them to return.

I walked around in a circle, staring up at the gated roof that allowed in light and air, and for a moment I was curious about what it was trying to keep out. I looked at Rhode, who was standing in the middle of my circle, watching me with a small grin on his face.

"What?" I asked, suddenly self-conscious.

"Nothing," he said softly. "I just love the light that comes to your eyes when you're curious about something."

"So, who are these Elders again?" Eris had done her best to explain the concept in the ride over, but my lack of sleep prevented me from paying attention and retaining all the information.

"They're the descendants of the original Salem witches. They fled during the witch trials and helped found the city of New Orleans. Their presence here has made New Orleans one of the largest magic communities in the country."

"So, why does no one talk about them?"

"They only meddle in events they feel bring danger to all witches."

"So, if they don't think that what Eris saw is important enough, then we're on our own?"

"That seems to be the situation at present, yes."

I looked up as Rhea, Eris, and Tennessee came into the courtyard, their faces a twisted mix of anxious and serious. "What happened?" My voice came out just as nerved as their faces looked. "What did they say?"

No one said anything as Rhea came up to me and took my hand in hers. "They would like to speak with you."

I gripped Rhea's hand hard as she led me to the large ceremonial chamber where the Elders were gathered. We walked into the center of a large pentagram, carved into the limestone floor, and at each point was a chair occupied by a woman in her early sixties. I looked at each point, gathering that an Elder of her element sat at her appointed corner of the pentagram.

"Is this her?" one of them asked. All of the elders wore black, but this one sat underneath the sigil of green with a mighty oak on it. An earth witch.

"Yes," Rhea answered. "This is Artemis."

"She had just been told of her lineage?" asked an Elder who sat under a sigil of blue with waves.

"Yes," Rhea answered, "about a week ago."

There was a small mutter of outrage before an Elder that sat under a sigil of amber with flames spoke. "Why was she not told sooner?"

"Our mother was murdered. My sister, Eris, and I felt the need to allow our family to grieve before we told Artemis what she was."

"There is nothing we can do," remarked the Elder that sat under the sigil of light blue with leaves on it.

"What do you mean there's nothing you can do?" asked Rhea, who was spitting mad at this conclusion.

"We sent the girl protection and that is all we can offer at this time," the air witch Elder continued.

"What your sister, Eris, saw does not pose a threat to the witch community as a whole," the water witch Elder said.

"That means you won't step in," I realized numbly, "because the Reapers are only after me."

"That is correct, child," the fire witch Elder said.

"What about the prophesy?" Rhea asked, her voice steady, but I could tell she was pleading and desperate for help.

I looked over at Rhea, slightly confused by what she had just said. "What are you talking about, Ray?"

"We have no way of knowing this child's true potential," the earth witch Elder said. "We simply cannot risk the lives of many for the life of one child, and a prophesy that may not even come to pass in this lifetime."

"There are Reapers in New Orleans, and you are going to do nothing?" Rhea countered. "It doesn't matter why they're here, they will kill as many witches as they can before they come for my sister."

"There have been Reapers in this city since it was first built," the earth witch Elder continued. "We have survived since then, and we will survive now."

"You are leaving us to the wolves and you know it!" Rhea walked away, clearly sick of talking to a group of Elders that had no intention of changing their minds.

I didn't follow my sister out of the circle; instead, I looked at the top point of the pentagram at the Elder who sat under a sigil of pure white. She hadn't spoken a word the entire time, just watched as everyone else spoke. I knew she was the spirit witch Elder, and that only she could answer my question.

I walked toward her, ignoring the sound of objection from the other Elders. I stood in front of her and said, "Just answer me this, if you can." She nodded as I pulled out a piece of paper and unfolded it in front of her, the face of the man I had been drawing staring her in the face. "Who is he?"

The spirit witch Elder looked at me with wide eyes as her face went white with fear. "He is the end of all we know," she said in a low voice.

"Apollo," I said softly.

She gave a nod, affirming what I had just said. "If this is truly what is coming, there is nothing that can be done to stop it. If you wish to survive, child, take your sisters and flee this city."

I stared her, knowing that she spoke the truth, knowing that it would soon all come to an end. I backed slowly out of the room, but I couldn't escape the chill that had settle in my bones.

✦◆◆)◦(◆◆✦

"WHAT CAN WE do next?" Rhode's voice rumbled.

After the meeting with the Elders, Rhea had insisted on leaving immediately and discussing nothing until we were in the car. I had been dead on my feet and had fallen asleep against Rhode before we even turned the street corner, but I hadn't fallen deep enough into sleep, so I could still make out what they were saying.

"We don't have many options," Tennessee said slowly. "The Elders have refused us sanctuary or intervention. At this point, our best chance is to take Artemis and run."

A long, tense silence filled the car. Would it have been so bad to run again? I had been doing it all of my life, bouncing from place to place, it wouldn't bother me if that was the life I had to live again. Not as long as my sisters and I were alive.

"It's okay, Ray," Eris voice said, breaking the terse feel that had fallen over the car. "She's just sleeping." I felt a soft touch sweep the hair from my face and another touch my hand and squeeze gently.

"I can't remember the last time she hasn't slept without tossing and turning or having to scream herself awake," Rhea said evenly. "This girl has had everything taken away from her and I'll be damned if we have to flee the only home she has left."

"Then our only option is to make a stand and fight, but we are outnumbered vastly by the Reapers," Tennessee said stiffly. "It's a death wish, Rhea."

"What am I supposed to do?" Rhea asked, her voice desperate and bordering on hysteric.

"We need to keep her safe," Eris said evenly. "We'll go to Izzy's and wait for things to die down, but for now that is the only option that keeps us alive."

I didn't hear anything else as I dropped off and fell further into sleep.

Chapter 15

"**A**rtemis," a voice wafted through my ear, so soft and so sweet that it didn't seem real.

I groaned at the sound and felt my head resting against my arms and my arms against something hard. I must have fallen asleep at the kitchen table again. It was a habit I had started to develop, but I had no idea why.

A hand stroked my hair gently, making me stir again. "Mom?" I mumbled, not entirely sure if I was still dreaming or not.

"Wake up, little bird," Mom's voice called sweetly.

I picked up my head and opened my eyes, only to come face to face with the murderous gaze of a Reaper, those haunting blue eyes damn near glowing behind his mask. I tried to run, but it grabbed the back of my neck and held fast, insuring I wouldn't escape whatever fate he had for me.

He held up the throwing knife I had used to stab him in the woods, the red blood now rusted and brown on the blade as he held it up in the light.

"I believe I owe you this back," he said before plunging the knife into my stomach.

I opened my mouth to let out a scream, but only air rushed out of my mouth with no sound behind it. I looked at him as I breathed a shaky breath, seeing my breath in the air as an icy chill began to settle into the air. The Reaper stared at me for a long moment, blue eyes meeting blue and, without a word, he twisted the blade.

I was screaming at the top of my lungs before I even realized I had woken up. It took everything within me to stop myself from screaming, but even now I knew it wouldn't be long before everyone came rushing in to see what had frightened me. I sat up in bed and let out a long and shaky breath, pushing my hands through my sweat-soaked hair as I tried to compose myself.

"I'm in my room," I muttered to myself, guessing that Tennessee or Rhode must have carried me up here once we had returned from the Elders. "I'm home and I'm safe."

"Artemis," the Reaper's voice crept past my ear and I flinched, covering my ears as I tried to shut him out desperately.

"You're not real," I whispered.

"Oh, I'm very real," he answered, his voice becoming firmer and louder.

I looked up and saw him standing there at the end of my bed, wearing that long black coat and faceless white mask that left only the eyes uncovered. I knew behind it was a murderous smile.

"You're not real," I said again, trying desperately to keep my resolve.

"I'll be seeing you very soon, Artemis," he said in an amused tone.

I picked up the half-full glass of water from the night stand beside me and threw it at him in a fit of anger I had no control over. The glass passed straight through him and shattered against the wall.

"You're not real!" I shrieked, closing my eyes, feeling my heart nearly explode in my chest. After a moment, I released the breath that I hadn't even realized I'd been holding and opened my eyes. The Reaper was gone.

I sagged against the bed, almost passing out. This Reaper didn't want to just kill me, I was realizing that now, he wanted to play games with my head. He wanted to break me down mentally before he finally carried out whatever plan he had for me. It was just a game to him.

I fell over onto my side, completely drained as the door opened and Eris and Rhode came running into the room. Eris got onto the bed, turning me over onto my back, and looked down into my eyes as I struggled to keep my breathing in check.

"Artemis, honey?" Eris called out as she shook me, trying to bring me back to the real world. "Artemis? Talk to me!"

My labored breathing was now coming in short gasps and I knew what this was. "Can't breathe," I gasped, my scared eyes looking into Eris's.

"Shit," she swore silently. "She's having a panic attack."

"A panic attack?" Rhode asked.

"She started having them after the accident," Eris explained. "She had one at school the day she passed out, but this one is really bad. I need you to help her while I got get her medication."

"Help her? How?"

"Figure it out, spirit witch," Eris said before climbing off the bed and leaving the room.

"It's okay," Rhode said, lifting me up. He sat behind me on the bed, allowing my body to lie against his like he had in the car this morning. He wrapped his arms around me tightly and leaned his face against mine as he rocked me back and forth, whispering over and over into my ear that it was okay.

"This is what happened that day in history when you passed out," he realized softly.

I nodded, but I was shaking too hard to know if that's what Rhode saw. "Shadows," I stammered.

"Shadows?" he asked, confused.

I wanted to explain, but I couldn't seem to get myself together enough to formulate an entire sentence. As if Rhode knew this was upsetting me, he placed his hand on my chest as I struggled to get breath into my lungs. "Rhode," I gasped.

"Just feel my breathing, darlin'," he said softly into my ear. "Just close your eyes and listen to me breathe. In and out."

I closed my eyes and listened, trying desperately to match my breathing with his long deep breaths that seemed so effortless to him. I reached up and placed my hand over his as we sat in silence for I don't know how long, just breathing.

Eris returned after not too long and sat on the bed in front of us. "Alright babe, you know what's going to happen now."

I nodded, opening my mouth to take the pill, feeling a tension in my chest as it traveled down. The tension lessened after a few minutes and soon I was feeling my ability to breathe ease.

"Tick, tock," the Reaper's voice said, my heart rate shooting back up through the roof as the fear returned. "I'll see you soon, Artemis."

I gasped, trying not to scream, and soon I was sobbing hysterically. "Get him out of my head!" I sobbed, unable to control my rush of emotions.

I felt Eris's arms around me as she pulled herself in, trying her best to comfort me. "Shh, it's okay now. You're okay now, little bird."

Only that was a lie. We all knew that. No one was okay now, and if this Reaper had his way, no one would make it out of this alive.

After I had calmed down, Eris instructed Rhode to go run me a bath to try and help relax me while the medication took effect. Rhode did as he was told, and Eris helped me to the bathroom where she stripped me and helped me into the tub.

"Just relax," she said. "I'll come check on you in a little while." She turned to Rhode before she left and said in a low voice, hoping that I wouldn't hear. "Stay with her, don't leave her alone."

"I'm not going to slit my wrists in the tub, Eris," I joked humorlessly. "Not again, anyways."

Eris didn't say anything, she only cleared her throat and, in that moment, I knew I had crossed a line with her.

"I'm sorry," I said quietly.

"It's okay. I'll be back to check on you." She left, closing the door behind her.

Rhode sat down on the floor with his back against the tub, giving me a bit of privacy as I washed. "Are you going to tell me what that was about?" he asked after a long moment.

"This would be the one and only time I will allow you to ask me the question that you wanted to ask when we first met," I said softly.

"Did you try to kill yourself?" Rhode asked after some hesitation.

"Yes," I answered honestly. "Six months ago, I was taking a bath and I slit my wrist in the tub. Set back my recovery quite a bit to say the least."

"Why?"

"I was sad." That was my only explanation for it. "I had just hit a really bad low and I decided that I didn't want to live like this anymore. I didn't want to be numb and broken anymore. I was sick of being a burden on my sisters and seeing that look of sadness in their eyes when they looked at me. So, while Rhea was at work and Eris was making lunch, I put a kitchen knife to my wrist and, you know the rest."

"Eris found you?"

"She did, blamed herself for it for a good month before I let her know that it wasn't her fault. I had a lapse and even if she was watching me 24/7, I would have found a way to try to do it one way or another. That incident is the reason she's always asking if I'm okay or if I'm hungry or trying to anticipate my wants and needs. She's determined to make sure that I never go back to that mindset."

"Have you?" he asked. "Gone back to that mindset since then?"

"A couple of times," I admitted, "but I try and remember that if I follow through I'll be breaking my sisters' hearts." I paused and looked up at the ceiling as I sunk lower into the water for a moment, knowing that if I even looked like I was going to drown myself, Rhode would pull me out. He'd probably hate me after so that, too. "The semicolon means that my story isn't over. I got it three months after I did this because after seeing the look on my sisters' faces at the hospital after I woke up, it was my wakeup call that I couldn't be selfish. I had to fight and I had to continue."

We sat there in silence so long that I lost track. I reached my hand from the edge of the tub to rest gently on Rhode's shoulder. He reached up his hand to touch mine, giving it a gentle squeeze.

"It wasn't a vision this time," I said finally.

Rhode turned around to look at me but I kept my eyes cast upwards. "What do you mean?"

"I could feel the knife slide into my stomach. I could feel his breath on mine. It was so real. It couldn't have been vision. That Reaper could get inside my head and he could project what he wanted me to see, he could manipulate it."

"What does that mean for us?"

"I have no idea, but it can only end badly."

We stopped talking after that and the medication didn't take long before it started making my eyes droop. Eris came back to check on me, helping me out of the tub and getting me dressed; I was too far gone to complain. It wasn't new for Eris, back when I was out to lunch, she had done this more times than I can count.

She walked by my side as I seemed to sleepwalk down the hall, relishing in the doped haze I was in, enjoying it while I still could.

I paused at my bedroom door but didn't reach to open it. Even though I knew someone had cleaned up the mess from the glass of water I'd thrown, I still knew the beds of my sheets were tangled up with the nightmares I kept having.

Eris took my arm and we kept walking passed my room. "You can sleep in my bed tonight, little bird."

"Eris," I started, but I was too out of it to protest.

Instead I let her lead me into her room and settle me down into her bed; her sheets were soft cotton that smelled like sunshine and wildflowers. I smiled as my head hit the pillow, feeling warmth wash over me as Eris covered me with the blankets.

"You hungry?" Eris asked, sitting down on the bed and stroking my hair calmly.

"No," I said, feeling myself slip away. "I just want to sleep."

"Okay. Get some sleep," she said softly, leaning over to kiss me on the cheek. "We'll talk when you wake up."

I was too far gone to respond, and I was out before Eris closed the door behind her.

Chapter 16

I couldn't remember what the nightmare was by the time I had fought my way back to consciousness. All I knew was that I awoke screaming and crying like I had more times than I ever wanted to in my lifetime.

It took me a moment to come back to where I was. I was still sleeping in Eris's bed—still scared to sleep in my own bed, even though it had been three days since the day we went to the council. The day that Reaper got into my head and terrified me down to my very core.

I got out of the bed and made my way down to the living room. The sun was still sleeping and I knew everyone else in the house was still sleeping too, despite my screaming. I sat down on the couch and turned on the TV, watching a late-night infomercial for something that seemed too stupid for anyone to buy.

I didn't move when I heard the creak from the bottom of the stairs, knowing that someone would come to check on me sooner or later. Someone always did. I cast a look over to Rhode who was coming over to the couch where he sat next to me.

"Talk to me," he said softly. "Please, darlin', just talk to me."

"I don't want to talk about it," was all I said.

"You know you have a look in your eyes when you've had a bad dream. This shadow behind your eyes, I see it there each and every time you wake up screaming in the middle of the night."

I kept my eyes glued to the TV as he talked, not wanting to talk about, refusing to give it the kind of power that made it too real.

"At least tell me if you're okay," he said slowly.

"No," I bit out sharply, "I'm not fucking okay. I wake up screaming every night from nightmares that I sometimes can't even remember. I'm a nervous wreck, I can't focus on anything and I'm expected to try and deal with all of this shit that's happening with the Reapers, but I can't." I fell off for a second as my voice broke. "I can't because I feel like I'm falling apart, Rhode."

Before I could say or do anything else, he moved over to where I was sitting and wrapped me up in his arms. I was so stunned by what had happened that I wasn't sure what to say. Rhode spoke instead. "Just let it out, darlin'," he whispered, holding me tight.

I wanted to push him away and tell him that I didn't need his pity. I wanted to be mad at him, but all I could do instead was unleash a flood of tears I didn't think I had in me. I let go and cried myself out as Rhode held me in the light of the TV, the infomercial still playing in the background.

After nothing was left to cry out and I'd pulled myself together, Rhode and I just sat there on the couch together, Rhode holding me and wrapping me in his comfort, and I allowed him to do so.

A few hours later I could hear footsteps moving around from upstairs, the sounds of Eris, Rhea, and Tennessee getting ready to come downstairs. I moved away from Rhode at the sound of footsteps descending the stairs, curling up against the armrest as Eris came into the living room, looking at the two of us slowly.

"You two are up early," she said quietly.

"Couldn't sleep," I said softly.

Eris only nodded at that, knowing exactly what had happened. "Come on in the kitchen. I'll get you two some breakfast while we wait for the others."

Slowly, I stood up off the couch and went into the kitchen with Eris, Rhode right behind me. I sat at the table and Eris poured us both a bowl of cereal, something I've only seen her do after she had had a rough night herself.

I didn't say anything about it as she set a bowl in front of each of us, sitting in the chair next to me and trying not to look like she was watching me closely. Rhode dug in, while I ate slowly, mostly moving the food around rather than eating it, but I made sure to eat a bite or two every once in a while so Eris wouldn't lecture me.

We were almost done eating when Tennessee and Rhea came into the kitchen, determined looks on the faces. The two of them had definitely been talking about the situation at hand, and clearly it had been in depth.

"Ten and I had a long talk," Rhea said quietly, her tone edgy. She came over and stood beside me, placing her hand on my shoulder. "We need to go back to the Elders."

"They've already given us their answer," I countered, confused by the sudden need to go back. "What else can we do to get them to help us?"

"Nothing," Eris answered, her voice sounded tired. "The only thing we can do now is run."

"If we run, they'll follow us," Rhea countered. "We need to find a way to end this. We owe it to Artemis to try."

"Ray, I'm fine," I said, but I'm sure the rough look on my face and weariness in my voice told a completely different story.

"You are not fine," she said firmly, squeezing my shoulder gently. "I haven't seen you like this since Mom died. You're not eating, you're barely sleeping, and when you do sleep, you wake up screaming from nightmares. I'm worried and I'm scared." Rhea paused and I could hear her fighting back tears. "God, I will not risk losing you again! The Elders know something that they aren't telling us and we are going to find out what."

"It can't hurt to asked again," Eris conceded, seeing the determination in Rhea's eyes. "Artemis will be safe with Rhode while we go and talk to them."

My eyes started to get heavy and I lost track of the conversation. I was almost pulled under to sleep when the voice of the Reaper whispered across my mind.

Tick tock, witch. Your time is almost up.

I gasped, feeling my heartrate shoot through the roof as I forced myself back to the surface as if I had been drowning under water and I was fighting to keep myself above water.

Everyone's eyes were on me, finally seeing how the lack of sleep had gotten to me after all these days. Eris reached out and cupped my cheek with her hand. "How much sleep did you get last night?"

I shook my head, not really sure myself. "Three, maybe four hours."

"You need to get some sleep," she said softly, getting up from the table and going out of sight somewhere.

"The three of us are going to go back and speak to the Elders," Rhea explained, "see if we can get anything else from them. Rhode, you stay here with Artemis."

Rhode nodded, serious in his task of guarding me.

Eris came back over to the table, took my hand in hers and looked up at me with a small smile as she set a cup of tea on the table in front of me. "I don't want tea," I said, hearing the irritability in my own voice from the lack of sleep.

"I know," she said softly. "This is special tea, this will help you sleep."

"I don't want to sleep, either."

"This will help with that. Deep sleep, no dreams."

I looked at her, at cup in front of me, and then at her again. "No dreams?"

Eris shook her head. "None."

I was so tired that I caved, knowing it wouldn't be long before I was dead on my feet and I dropped from exhaustion anyway. I took a few swallows of the tea, and it wasn't long before I felt a warmth spread through me and I knew it was working.

"How long will it take?" I asked, my lips barely moving.

"Not long," Eris whispered, running her fingers through my hair. My eyes were so heavy, I couldn't keep them open anymore. I gave into the warmth and let my eyes fall all the way closed, falling over as though all my strength left me. "Sleep well, little bird," Eris whispered.

That was the last thing I heard before the world went dark.

Chapter 17

I don't know how long it was before I finally surfaced from what felt like a coma. I opened my eyes slowly, seeing that I was lying on the couch again. Rhode was sitting in an arm chair in the corner, watching me as I slept; he must have carried me back into the living room after I'd fallen under.

"Hey," he said when he saw I was finally awake.

"Hey," I said softly as my senses started to fully return to me.

"How did you sleep?"

I sat up on the couch and ran my hand through my ruffled hair. "No dreams." Eris, always true to her word, had given me something that made me seem dead to the world.

"Eris said to make sure you ate when you got up," Rhode said, ducking into the kitchen and coming back with a big bowl of tomato soup and a grilled cheese sandwich. He set the food on the coffee table in front of me and explained the situation at hand as I tore into the food with a ravenous hunger I hadn't felt in a long time.

"So, they went to see if the Elders can do anything more," I said bluntly as I finished the last of my soup.

Rhode nodded. "Rhea wanted to give it one more try in case they're hiding something from us."

Something in my gut told me they were, but what they were hiding didn't have to do with the Reapers. "What if they get the same answer?"

"We pack up and run until we can figure out another plan."

"This city isn't safe anymore," I said numbly. "We should have left a long time ago."

Rhode took my hand in his and gently squeezed. "Everything will be okay. Nothing is going to happened to you, Artemis, I promise you that."

He leaned in closer and I could see the amber flecks in his toffee-colored eyes. "I will make sure nothing happens to you," he said firmly, leaning in so that our lips brushed against one another.

I'm not sure who kissed who, but we felt a spark as we both started kissing back. I pulled away, breathless from the kissing and speechless by the act of the kiss itself. I smiled and touched my lips with my fingers, remembering his touch, and that made him smile.

I opened my mouth to say something, but a loud knock came from the door, scaring the ever loving shit out of me.

"I'll get it," I volunteered, getting up off the couch, but I could feel Rhode hold onto my hand, refusing to let got as he stared at the door. "I'll be fine, Rhode," I said softly, stepping forward as his grip loosened and my hand slid out. I went to the door, keeping the chain hooked and only allowing the door to swing open the length of the chain. "Caleb," I said in mild surprise as he leaned just outside my doorframe.

"Hey there, beautiful," he said, smiling that wolfish grin of his. "I've been calling you for days and you haven't been answering. I'm starting to get offended."

"Sorry," I apologized. "I've been dealing with a lot of stuff that's been going on recently."

"Jesus, you look like shit," he observed bluntly.

"Gee, thanks, you really know how to make a girl feel special."

"I just wanted to pop by and see you," he said in mock offense.

"Well, you've seen me," I noted, "so leave."

"What happened to you?" He leaned a little bit of his face into the small space that the door chain allowed. "You used to be a lot of fun."

"I told you, I'm going through some things. I'll see you later, Caleb," I said in a rush. I tried to close the door, but Caleb jammed his foot into the crack, making it impossible for me to get the door closed.

"Can I come in?" he asked. "I've got some party favors that I think that you might like."

In one swift movement, Rhode had gone from the couch to the door and had wedged himself in front of me so that I could see Caleb face to face. "You need to leave," he said, his voice full of deadly malice. "Now."

"It seems you've made your choice," Caleb said softly. "Fair is fair I guess, seeing as I've already made mine."

The shatter of glass in the kitchen turned mine and Rhode's attention away from the door, giving Caleb his chance to shoulder it open. He landed right on top of Rhode and the two of them began to wrestle, trying to take the other down. Caleb quickly gained the upper hand and was on top of Rhode, punching him over and over again.

"Run," Rhode spat, blood flying from his mouth as another blow landed. "Artemis, run!"

I obeyed, taking off toward the stairs, which were my only option at this point. I had made it to the bottom of the stairs when the second Reaper that broken in through the back came in through the kitchen. He grabbed at me, but I scrambled up the stairs with him behind me. I ran for dear life and gave myself a second or two of a lead ahead of him, which in this case was life or death, making my way to the bathroom where I shut the door and locked it.

I hadn't even managed to take the next breath when the door shuttered behind me. I backed away, looking around the bathroom and trying to make a plan to save myself, because I knew that door wouldn't hold and that Reaper would be here in less than a minute. I closed my eyes and the light bulb went off. I went to the decorative basket full of hand towels on top of the sink and scoured through them, nearly doubling over with relief when I found my knife.

I meant what I had said to Rhode when I'd told him I'd gone to a bad mindset since the first time I tried to kill myself six months ago. What I hadn't told him was that I had stashed knives and razors all over the house for those days, including the hand basket that was for decoration and not for function. I thanked my lucky stars that no one had found it, because today, this knife was going to save my life rather than end it.

I saw the door start to splinter and I knew that it was almost time. I went over to the small nook behind by the door that we used for towels and braced myself against it. Closing my eyes, I heard the door disintegrate as the Reapers barreled through.

I stayed perfectly still as he came into the bathroom, looking around as if he expected to find a cowering child right there in front of him. "Where are you, bitch?"

I took careful steps toward him, making sure I was completely silent as I stepped up behind him and slit his throat. The initial spray of blood ended up on the walls as the Reaper grabbed his throat, making desperate choking sounds as the blood continued to spill out with no signs of stopping. He fell to the floor and I stood there and watched as his eyes went glassy and his breathing stopped altogether as he lay in a pool of his own blood on my bathroom floor.

I took a step back and spit on his body before I made my way back downstairs in the hopes that Rhode had ended Caleb. I carefully took the steps down as I heard the fighting in the living room continue. There were punching sounds and a high pitch whining that made my heart stop and my blood run cold.

"Come on out, Artemis!" Caleb shouted in an amused voice. "Or I'm afraid that I'll have to put your little pet down."

I heard Rhode's wolf howl in pain and I knew I couldn't let him die for me. I closed my eyes and let loose a shaky breath before stepping out of hiding and into the living room. Caleb looked up where he was crouched on the floor over Rhode's wolf that was lying unmoving on the floor, his eyes closed.

I held my hands up so he could see them, but refused to let go of the knife. "You win, Caleb." I looked at the unmoving wolf. "I'll go with you."

"I'm glad you see it my way," he said, a cocky smiling proving he was relishing the moment.

"One condition," I amended. "I call Rhode's brother and get him help."

"I really don't think you're in a position to bargain here, sweetheart."

I held the knife to my wrist and angled it over a vein, proving to Caleb that I knew exactly what I was doing. "I think that I am," I countered.

Caleb's smile fell and I could see the look of contempt now forming on his face. "I assume that if I went upstairs then I would find a dead body?"

I didn't say anything, I let my sinister smile and the blood-coated knife do the talking for me.

"Make your call," he said. "You might as well get a chance to say your goodbyes."

I flipped him off before I took my phone out of my pocket, dialing Tennessee's number, knowing that he would be the calmest about this situation.

"Hello?"

"Ten, you need to come home right now. Rhode's hurt."

"Hurt? What's going on, Artemis?"

"I'm being taken and I won't be here by the time you make it back. Just get here and save Rhode," I said softly, my voice breaking a little, "don't let him die because of me."

"Artemis," Tennessee said in a tense tone.

"Tell Rhea and Eris that I love them," I cried, "tell them that I didn't have a choice, okay?"

"We will find you, little witch," Tennessee promised. "There's no need for goodbyes."

"I know you will," I whispered. "I just wanted to say it . . . just in case." I hung up the phone without another word, because I knew I would start bawling if Rhea or Eris got on the phone and then I wouldn't be able to go through with this. I had to, I had to do this so Rhode could have a chance to live, even if I didn't.

"Toss the phone," Caleb bit out.

I tossed the phone toward the stairs, hearing my lifeline skitter away in an instant.

"Now the knife," he said, taking a step closer to me.

I walked slowly over to Rhode's wolf and placed the knife down. I took my locket from around my neck, placing a kiss to it before I left it next to the knife. "I know you will find me," I whispered to the wolf. "I know it." I placed a kiss to his head and stood up, facing Caleb.

Caleb stepped closer to me, brushing my hair over my shoulder in a move that made me shudder. "You should have stuck with me, Artemis. I might have been able to convince them to spare your life."

I looked at him with dead eyes. "You're a stupid boy who doesn't know what he's gotten himself into. Those men will never listen to you or bend to you or grant you favors. Now that you've served your purpose, you'll be lucky to keep your life."

Caleb's face hardened and went sour. "I was going to give you the drugs to put you out," he said coldly, "but I think I'm going to enjoy the alternative."

Before I could react, he grabbed me by the hair and bashed my face into the wall.

Lights out.

Chapter 18

I awoke with a start to my face really fucking hurt. I automatically reached to touch it, but my arms wouldn't move. Dazed, I looked up to see that my wrists had been bound together over a pipe that ran along the ceiling. My toes barely touched the floor and I could feel my shoulders being torn from the weight of hanging there.

"So, this is the bitch that everyone's making such a fuss about?"

I jerked to see a Reaper standing in front of me, looking at me with curiosity and hatred in his eyes.

"It seems so," the one beside him said evenly.

"She doesn't look like much."

"That's what we thought, but Caleb tells us that she sliced open Logan's throat. Clean through, no hesitation. Girl's a stone-cold killer."

"Never underestimate the rage of a seventeen-year-old girl, eh?"

The second one grunted and left the first one's side, out of my view, but I could hear him rustling around behind me.

"Alright sweetheart, here's how it's going to go. I'm going to ask you some questions, and for every one you answer, you'll remained unharmed. For every one that you don't . . ." He gestured behind me to something I couldn't see that made him smile in such a sick way. "My friend is going to do something that I don't think you're going to like very much. Do you understand?"

I nodded.

"Good, let's start off with an easy one. What's your name?"

"Artemis," I said softly.

The Reaper smiled with a bit of satisfaction. "Good. What kind of witch are you?"

"What are you talking about?" I hoped that if I played dumb, the

Reapers would have thought that I didn't know anything and let me go. It was a really, really long shot, but I had to try.

The Reaper walked up to me, even with the mask I could tell he was much older than his partner. He had cloudy gray eyes and salt and pepper hair. He came face to face with me and my guess was that he was roughly my height, as well.

He took my chin roughly between his thumb and forefinger, forcing me to look at him as he stared me down for a long moment. "You're lying," he concluded, back-handing me across the face so suddenly I almost hadn't realized what had happed. "Next time you lie to me, it won't be so nice. Now answer the question."

I looked up at him in utter surprise and shock at what he had just done, "I don't . . . I don't know."

The Reaper looked at me for another moment. I don't know if it was the fear in my eyes or if he saw something else. "What about your sisters? I'm sure you know what type of witches they are."

I looked up at him. "You leave my sisters out of this," I hissed at him.

The Reaper made a tsking noise with his tongue before signaling the Reaper behind me. The second Reaper came up behind me, quiet and stealthy. I felt his hand move up my back and I felt sick. His fingers stopped at the top of my neck as he gripped it tightly. I felt a shock rip through my body as if I had been struck by lightning.

"I told you that if you lied to me again it wouldn't be very nice."

I hung there, my restraints being the only thing that kept me from collapsing to the floor as waves of pain rocked my body. I looked up as the Reaper circled around, cattle prod in hand. He had a smug look on his face as he saw me in pain. "Calm down, honey. That was just the lowest setting, won't do you much harm."

His partner took over from there. "Each time you lie to me or you refuse to answer my question, my partner here will turn up the voltage. Now tell me about your sisters' magic."

I took my time, pulling myself up so that I was eye level with him. "I don't know," I answered in a low voice, prepared to face the consequences of what I had done. Even if it meant torture for me, at the very least I could keep my sisters safe from the Reapers.

"Pity," was all he said before I felt the cattle prod connect and pain slice through my flesh. "Care to change your answer?" he asked, offering me one last reprieve.

"Fuck you," I spat, only to be rewarded with another jolt of voltage racking my body and robbing me of what little strength I had. I groaned, biting my tongue to keep from crying out in pain. I refused to give those assholes the satisfaction.

"We'll try again tomorrow," he said quietly as he and the other Reapers went to the door and left, shutting me alone in the room with only my thoughts.

After I was sure they had left, I tried to swing my feet over the pipe so I could try and undo my ties. I'd failed for more than an hour, I think, before finally wearing myself out and falling asleep.

I didn't get much sleep before the door opened again and two Reapers entered the room. I had no clue if they were the same as last time, since the Reapers always wore those white masks.

"Hello again, sweetheart." The familiar chilling tone of the first Reaper affirmed that he was indeed the same who'd tortured me last time. The second Reaper was different, though, taller and more muscle-bound. "We're going to try again with those questions."

The first Reaper stood off to the side as the second stood in front of me, cracking his knuckles. This was going to be a long day, I could just fucking tell.

"I have to use the bathroom," I croaked out, my mouth dry. I hadn't been fed or given water since being taken, and I could tell this had been done with a purpose.

"Bathroom?" the first Reaper asked in offense. "You've got a bathroom all around you, sweetheart, but I could be persuaded to make arrangements if you were to give me the information that I need."

So that was a hard no, since I didn't have any information to give, and I definitely wouldn't have given him anything if I did. "Who's in charge here?" I asked, playing any card I could think of to try and stop this interrogation. "I want to speak to whoever is in charge of all this."

The Reaper's face ticked in a small smile. "Trust me, you don't want to see the boss. Only time people meet him is when they're about to die. He wasn't too taken with your behavior yesterday either, gave me permission to up the ante a little."

"I suppose we should get this show on the road." I sighed. "Ask away."

"I do believe you when you tell me you don't know what kind of witch you are. Care to take a guess?" he asked me emotionlessly.

"I'm a witch that has to go to the fucking bathroom," I said, closing my eyes. A heartbeat later I felt the fist of the second Reaper make contact with my face.

"You can make this stop, Artemis," the first Reaper said. "All you have to do is say something, so I'll ask again."

He could ask until his face turned blue, in fact, he did, asking question after question about me and Mom and my sisters and the Guardians the Elders had sent to protect me, but I refused to give in and told him nothing. Each time I refused to answer, the burly Reaper continued to hit me, moving from the face down my body to my ribs and my back. I took everything he gave me, refusing to cry out for mercy or for them to stop or be in pain. I would have rather died in pain than give them an ounce of satisfaction.

"Come, witch," the first Reaper said as I hung from the pipe by my ties, weak and bloody and near passing out. "You're only making things worse for yourself."

"Fuck. You," I said weakly with a dark chuckle. The next hit was so hard, I thought I actually saw stars around my head. "Rhode," the name escaped my mouth before I even realized it.

"Stop!" the first Reaper cried, pushing the second aside and coming very close to me, taking my chin in his hand and forcing me to look up at him. "What did you say?"

My eyes shut from the weakness. "Rhode," I mumbled again, not knowing if I was calling out for him or if I just wanted his name to be the last thing on my lips.

The Reaper let go of me. "You idiot, you hit her too hard! Now she's just mumbling nonsense."

I couldn't understand anymore of the words they were saying. All I could hear was the sound of boots on the floor and the door closing.

Then the world fell away.

I WAS STANDING in the living room of my house in New Orleans again and I nearly cried at the cruel trick my dreams were playing on me. I looked into the kitchen and saw Eris, Rhea, and Tennessee around the table. None of them had looked like they had gotten any sleep, especially Rhea who was pacing around the kitchen nervously.

"It's been two days," she said anxiously. "Why is this taking so long?

"I told you they have wards up, Rhea," Eris explained. She sat at the table holding something that looked like a map. "The Reapers don't want us to find them. All I know is that they're still in the state. The rest is going to take time."

"Where is she?"

I turned and saw that Rhode had come down the stairs and was standing at the kitchen door.

Everyone's attention had turned to him as he stood there, holding his ribs, some of which were probably broken. His face was still bruised but looked to be quite a bit healed from his fight with Caleb, and I nearly collapsed at all he had sacrificed in the name of protecting me.

"Hey, little brother," Tennessee said softly, going over to him and placing a hand gingerly on his shoulder. "How are you feeling?"

"Where is she?" Rhode asked again, his voice deadly and determined.

Tennessee gave Rhode's shoulder a gently squeeze. "We're looking for her. We're going to find her, Rhode. I promise you that."

Rhode nodded, his resolve falling as he allowed Tennessee to lead him to the table. "How long have I been out?" he asked, sitting down next to Eris as Tennessee remained standing.

"Couple of days," Tennessee said softly. "I thought I'd lost you back there."

Rhode smirked a little. "You can't get rid of me that easily, big brother."

"I'll make you something to eat," he said, ruffling Rhode's hair. "Help you get your strength back up."

I came in closer to see what Eris was doing. She was holding the locket that I had left behind over a map of the state of Louisiana. I watched curiously as the locket swung around and around at a slow pace, but it never stopped.

"It's a tracking spell," I realized, the light bulb going off that this wasn't a dream or a hallucination. I had managed to project my subconscious back to the house. This was happening now, in the present. I decided to go for broke and test how far this magic could get me before it was gone and I was back in the basement with my captors. "Rhode," I breathed, my breath shuttering as his head suddenly turned in my direction. "Can you see me?"

"Artemis?" Rhode's eyes went wide as he stood up, using the table to brace myself.

The entire kitchen fell silent as everyone looked to where I was standing in the kitchen. Rhea ran over to me. "Artemis," she cried out, only to shed more tears when she saw my black and purple face covered in bruises. She reached out as if to check them, but her hand only passed through, much to her dismay.

"You're not really here," she said, her voice broken by that realization.

I shook my head. "No, I'm not. I don't know what's happening or how I'm doing this, but I don't think it will last long." I looked over at Eris. "You're using my locket for a tracking spell?"

Eris nodded. "I'm trying, but whatever they have blocking me is too strong. I don't know how long it will take the spell to find where you are."

"Do you know where you are?" Tennessee asked. "Have you seen any kind of clue to where you're being held?"

I shook my head. "Caleb knocked me out and I woke up in a basement. There aren't any windows down there and I'm tied up so I can't see out the door for a way out."

"It's okay," Tennessee said calmly. "Eris's plan will work, we can use the tracking spell to find you. It's just going to take some time."

"Rhode can do it," I said softly as the puzzle pieces came together.

"What?" Rhode looked at me confused.

"Your wolf is bonded to me," I explained. "You can use your wolf's bond to break the wards and find me with the tracking spell."

Everyone looked from me to Rhode to Eris who said, "Hell, it's worth a shot."

She slid the map in front of Rhode and handed him my locket. We all stood around as Rhode held the locket over the map, the pendant making steady circles before it finally landed on an area. I was somewhere just outside the city, in the woods or something by the looks of it.

"It worked," Rhode breathed.

Everyone was just as shelled shocked as him. "Good," I breathed, hoping they would have found me before the Reapers took their tactics of questioning to a brand-new level.

Rhode stood up and came over to me, those beautiful, toffee-colored eyes of his piercing mine. "We know where you are and we're going to find you, I promise. You just need to hang on until then, just hang on Artemis."

"I know you'll find me," I managed, feeling myself fading. I looked over at Eris and Rhea and offered them a small smile. "I love you guys."

"We love you, too, little bird," Eris said.

"Just hang on," Rhea pleaded, "we're coming for you, Artemis."

I was gone after that, waking up in the same cold, dark basement I'd been in for the past two days. Jesus, had it really been that long? I closed my eyes and tried to calm myself with the fact that my sisters knew where I was and they were coming for me. I just had to make sure I survived until then.

Chapter 19

When I woke up, the Reapers had already entered the room. The first one sat in front of me with a plate of fried chicken that made me sag as I realized how weak with hunger I was. "Good morning, sweetheart," he said, beginning his good cop routine. "Hungry?"

I said nothing.

"I see you finally caved and pissed yourself. Held out a whole two days, though, that's a record around here I think. Most witches piss themselves in terror their first hour. Good on you, sweetheart."

I turned my head a little as I heard a small rustle of the other Reaper moving behind me. Before I could track his movements, he appeared in front of me. "Hello there," he said with a strong Sothern drawl. "My name's Jeb."

I didn't say anything in response.

"You don't talk much, do you darlin'?" I squirmed underneath his hands as they traveled up and down my body. "Sure, you do. I'm sure when a man touches you just right." I nearly cried out as his had groped my breast. "You call out his name plenty."

I looked up at the ceiling, closing my eyes as his hands went down farther. The second his hand was between my thighs, I used every ounce of energy I had to lift my bound legs and try to kick Jeb in the groin.

"Whoa there," he said, backing up out of my reach as I tried desperately to kick him. "We got a wild little filly here, don't we?" He stepped forward, taking my hips and forcing me to stop moving. "My friend over there is going to ask you some questions. You answer, then you might get some food, and maybe we'll have a little fun. Keep up this little act you've been doing and you ain't going to like the consequences."

Jeb disappeared from view and the first Reaper appeared, holding up the plate of food in front of my face so I could smell it. My stomach growled in response, but I had to keep myself mentally strong if I was going to try and get out of this place intact.

"Are you going to answer my questions today?" He waved the food in front of my face like he would wave a bone in front of a dog to make him beg.

"I think we know each other well enough by now that you know the answer," I said simply.

"That's what I thought," he said with a nod, and I could hear Jeb behind me as the first Reaper took his seat again. "The guys are sick of you playing games, and they've decided that if I can't get anything out of you today, then we're going to have no further use for you, witch. They've also given me Jeb, who is very persuasive in the department."

"You can torture me all you want, but you will get nothing from me."

"Of, of that I have no doubt," he said with darkness in his voice. "This is for my satisfaction, pure and simple."

I heard Jeb's footsteps come up behind me, and I could feel a low heat against my skin that was getting warmer and warmer. "You know what we do to a wild filly on the farm? We brand 'em."

I broke my vow to myself, screaming out in pain as I felt the searing hot metal touch the flesh on my back.

"Scream all you want, sweetheart," the Reaper said, "no one can hear you, and even if they could, no one is coming to your rescue."

By the time Jeb stepped back, I was gasping in ragged breaths and about to pass out from the pain, but I just couldn't. I looked up at the first Reaper, expecting him to ask me another question, but he simply sat there watching me.

"I had a long talk with the boss and he isn't happy with you or with me. I figured that if I'm going to burn because of you, I could get a bit of my own satisfaction out of the process."

Jeb stepped into my view and I could see the brand he was holding, some kind of coat of arms with lions on it. "The brand of the Reapers," Jeb explained. "Every Reaper had the mark tattooed on their skin when they are officially inducted into the Reapers."

"We also use it to mark the witches we kill," the first Reapers explained. "Let the rest of your kind know what we did."

"Why are you telling me this?"

"You finally get your wish, little filly," Jeb said. "You get to meet the big boss tomorrow."

The first Reapers stood up and looked at me for a moment. "Such a disappointment," he remarked. "It'll be a shame to have to dispose of you in the morning." With that, he and Jeb walked out of the room, the door closing behind them with a damning click.

"Eris and Ray are coming," I muttered to myself, "they're coming and they're going to find me. They will."

The only question now was were they going to find me alive?

Chapter 20

The pain and hunger had finally caught up with me and I passed out for a little while. I was jerked awake when the door opened again and I saw a lone Reaper come into the room.

"If you put your dick anywhere near me, I swear to the Virgin Mary herself I will bite it off."

"Jesus, you're a crass one," a familiar voice said sharply.

"Caleb?" I asked in shock. "Fuck off, you can go ahead a kill me right now asshole, I'm not letting you touch me."

Caleb took off his mask and looked at me with a little smirk on his face, like he was an action hero. "No one's dying tonight."

"What are you doing here?" I asked as he started untying my feet.

"I'm attempting a daring rescue at the expense of my own life. Jesus, what does it look like?"

"Why are you helping me?"

Caleb came up behind me and placed his hands around my hips. "I'm going to lift you now and it's going to hurt like hell, okay?"

I nodded and Caleb lifted up and over an open part of the pipe. He was right, too, all the damage that had been done to me over the past few days had taken its toll and the pain was too much. I couldn't help but cry out.

"It's okay," Caleb whispered in my ear as he lowered my feet to the ground. Unfortunately, my strength was long gone and I couldn't hold myself up. I sank to the floor without hesitation. "Easy, easy," Caleb murmured as he helped me to the ground.

"You didn't answer my question," I said wearily as Caleb untied my wrists. "Why are you helping me?"

Caleb looked me in the eye and said evenly, "I may have sold my soul to the devil when I signed up with the Reapers, but I did not sign up to kill people."

"You tell that to Danny," I hissed.

"I didn't want that to happen to Danny, and now that his blood is on my hands, I refuse to stain it with yours, Artemis." He reached into his coat and pulled out his hunting knife, handing it to me.

"What am I supposed to do?" I took the handle of the blade, the memory of the first Reaper I had killed back at the house rushing through me.

"You've got two choices before that door opens again and those Reapers come in to torture and kill you. Kill yourself and beat them to the punch, or you make your peace with whatever God you have and get ready to kill them. Here." He reached into the pocket of his coat and pulled out two EpiPens. "The adrenaline will help you for a while, at least until you can get help. I'll leave the door unlocked on my way out. One way or another, good luck."

"Thank you, Caleb," I said softly.

A ghost of a smile appeared on Caleb's face as he leaned in and kissed me on the forehead before getting up and disappearing out of the door as quickly as he had come.

I dragged myself over to a corner where it would have been harder to spot me by anyone that came in unexpectedly. I took sixty seconds and mentally prepared myself to kill each and every Reaper that got between me and my way out of this hell hole. I shot both EpiPens into my thigh and, once I felt the surge of adrenaline, I went.

The door was open, just as Caleb had promised, and behind it were ascending steps that went up to the kitchen. I looked around and saw I was in a house or a cabin somewhere in the middle of the woods.

I took my chances and bolted toward the door, only to come face to face with a Reaper that was coming into the kitchen from the adjacent room.

"What the fuck are you doing in here?" he growled.

I didn't give him time to sound an alarm, I stuck my knife in his throat and sliced as deep as I could. I said nothing as the spray hit me in my face, I simply took my chance and headed to the backdoor.

There were two more Reapers keeping watch at the backdoor, so I took a deep breath and, on the exhale, opened the door. I took the first one down immediately, slicing his throat open while the other was stunned that he was watching a teenage girl murder a Reaper. I went after him next, slicing right into his jugular before he had a chance to sound for help.

I didn't bother to see if any of them were dead. As soon as I dropped the Reapers outside, I ran straight toward the woods. I ran like a bat out of hell and didn't look back. I had probably made it a mile, maybe a mile and a half before I started to slow my pace, hopped up on the adrenaline rush that was now starting to fade.

I came to a full stop, nearly falling over when I heard the sound of a wolf howling into the night. I closed my eyes and listened to the sound echoing through the night—it was close. "Rhode!" I called out, making my way through the darkness toward the sound of howling.

The howling was extremely close, and I could see through the darkness the toffee-colored eyes that Rhode shared with his wolf. Tennessee followed right behind him, both a sight for sore eyes.

I dropped the knife and looked at him in completely shock. Was it really them or was I going to wake up screaming back in the basement again? "You found me?"

Tennessee walked over and took me into his arms, his strength and warmth making me sob with relief. "It's okay, little witch," he whispered in my ear as his hold on me tightened.

"I knew you'd find me," I sobbed. "I knew it!"

"We promised you we would." He pulled back and looked at me. I knew he was taking in the damage that three days of questioning by the Reapers had resulted in. "How long until the Reapers come looking for you?"

"Not long. I kind of left a trail of bodies at the cabin that they won't be very happy about."

"How many?" Tennessee asked, sincere curiosity in his voice.

"Three, four if you count the one I killed before I was taken."

"That a girl." He sighed, kissing the top of my head.

I looked up as figures moved from behind the trees, and I saw my sisters and almost collapsed in joy. Eris ran toward me, taking me from Tennessee and wrapping me in an embrace of her own. Rhea walked slowly to me, reaching out her hand as if she were afraid it would pass right through me. When our hands connected, I could see tears run down her face and she hugged both Eris and me.

"A touching family reunion," a chilling voice said from behind us. We turned to face the direction it had come and saw a large group of Reapers emerge from the direction I had just come from. "It's fitting really," he went on, "families should die together. Saves the grief." His eyes settled on me and my heart started beating even faster. "Then again, you did kill four of my men. Maybe I should kill your boyfriend first."

I looked at Rhode's wolf form in sheer panic, thinking back to seeing him lying near dead on my living room floor. I wasn't prepared to have gone through all this hell only to lose him all over again. I wasn't prepared to lose anyone again. The wolf made a firm stance in front of me, growling at the group of Reapers, making sure they knew they had to kill him to get to me.

"Or maybe a sister," he suggested, looking between Rhea and Eris and seeing the anger on my face. "Yes, a sister."

Without hesitation, Rhea stepped forward, standing firm as her offering to the Reapers. Stubborn and headstrong, just like the earth witch she was, ready to stand firm to this if it meant that her younger sisters could live.

"Do we have a volunteer?" the Reaper asked in an amused voice. "Kill the brave one first."

My gaze turned murderous, knowing they weren't going to let any of us out of here alive without a fight, and I was not going to watch my sister die. Catching sight of a Reaper stepping forward, I let out a primal scream and felt the world go blindly bright as I felt warmth spring from my chest and surround us.

When I opened my eyes, I saw several Reapers on the ground, or at least what was left of them; the figures on the ground had been scorched completely and turned to ashes. "Fire," I said numbly as I looked at my hand and could feel the light and warmth traveling through me. Rhea had been right, my magic presented itself at the right moment.

"Mom was right," Eris said in shock, "she's a fire witch."

"Explains a lot more growing up now that I think about it." Rhea sighed.

As the smoke cleared I could see that not all of the Reapers had gone down in my burst of magic. I saw three of them standing inside a large sphere of water being cast by one of the Reapers.

"He's a witch," I stammered as we looked on in disbelief. "Ray, that Reaper is a witch."

The sphere of water disappeared and the Reapers that he been standing to the right stepped forward, taking off his mask so I could see him fully. His long dark hair and sapphire blue eyes almost seemed to glow.

"Apollo," I said numbly, still able to recognize my twin brother in the flesh seventeen years later, even through all the shock.

"Hello big sisters," he said in a low voice, "it's been a long time."

"That means . . ." I trailed off as I looked past him to the man who had been standing next to Apollo.

He took off his mask and my heart froze as I saw those cold green eyes and the dark hair that both Rhea and I had also inherited.

"Dad?" Eris breathed in shock.

"Hello girls," he said with an evil smile. "My, how you've all grown."

"You're a Reaper," Rhea said with a dry and humorless laugh. "That makes too much sense. You married a witch and waited for her to give you a son so you could take him away from his family and raise him to hate his own kind. A Reaper with magic, what better tool is there for killing witches?"

"What do you want from me?" I asked. "Why have you come back after all this time? For what?"

"Isn't it obvious? The great prophesy the Elders never bothered to tell you. One twin born of love and the other of hate, your death ensures the rise of the Reapers while your twin's death ensures their fall."

I looked over to Rhea, whose face had gone pale in the mist of everything. "Is this what you meant when you asked the Elders about the prophesy?"

She nodded. "It was never a concern until we found out he was alive," she whispered in a shaky voice.

"It isn't too late," Dad offered. "Join me, my girls, and you will have a chance to survive what is to come." His eyes slide to Eris. "You've felt it, haven't you, Eris? You've felt the darkness that is coming to envelop you all."

"It won't happen," I said firmly. "We won't let it."

Dad simply nodded, the smile vanishing from his face, making him look hard and lethal. "Very well," he turned to looked at Apollo, "kill them all."

Before I was aware of it, Apollo and I were walking toward each other, my eyes locked onto his as we did so. "Don't do this, Apollo. Don't be his puppet." I took another step toward him as he took a step toward me, his face unreadable. "Come with us and choose your own path, your own destiny." We were standing inches apart, our eyes still locked onto each other. "Come with us and be a family."

Apollo's icy mask broke in that moment, and I thought I had finally reached him deep down in the dark prison of poison our father had infected him with.

"My dear sister," he said, soft enough that only I could hear. Apollo reached for me, placing a strong arm around my back and pulling me into him.

My eyes went wide as I felt a sharp pain as he pulled me into his embrace. It was like ice in the gut, but all I could feel was warmth spilling out of me, and I didn't know what was happening. I looked up at him, meeting Apollo's cold gaze as he watched the pain he had inflicted on me.

"Why?" I breathed out, my voice quaking.

"I have chosen my path, witch. I need no family of yours," he said in a dark voice, twisting the knife in my stomach with no remorse as I cried out in pain.

He released me and, without his grip to keep me steady, I stumbled backward a few feet. I looked down at the icy pain in my gut, seeing my hands come away red with blood still warm from my beating heart.

I ran my hand over the handle of the knife, feeling the familiar indentations of the grip, and I realized with bitterness that he had stabbed me with the same knife I had stabbed the Reaper with that night in the woods.

"I told you," he said in that voice that had haunted my dreams for so many nights. "I owed you that back."

I looked up at my twin brother in shock as he lifted up his shirt and I saw the stab wound in his gut; now there was an identical on in mine.

This young man can be your destruction or your salvation. Madame

Josephine's words echoed in my mind as everything started to click and make much more sense than it had the day before.

"Goodbye, my sister," Apollo said coldly.

Before he had the chance to strike first, I felt something course through me. Suddenly a ring of fire rose from the ground, encircling me and my family as the flames warded off anyone unwelcomed into the circle.

The fire didn't stop Apollo, but it did slow him down. He approached slowly, stopping just short of the fire as he watched me with those cold eyes that were mirrors of mine. He held out his hand into the flame for a moment or two before he pulled back, keeping eye contact with me so that I could see there was no pain in his eyes. He wanted me to know that even if my fire could hurt him, he would endure it, that's how much he wanted my death.

Dad walked to the edge of the circle, standing next to Apollo and putting up his hand to test the heat of the fire and the strength of it. "I'm impressed, Artemis," he said, and for a second I thought I heard pride in his voice. "You always were a late bloomer, but you always did surpass all that came against you."

"If you want to live, run. Run and don't ever darken our doorway again," I hissed, prepared to kill him in cold blood where he stood if it meant protecting the people that I loved.

"Your mother said the same thing to me on the day you were born. That didn't work out for her in the end either."

We locked eyes for a moment before Dad signaled the remaining Reapers to follow him away from us. They all fell back as soon as the order had been given, but Apollo stayed where he was at the edge of the circle.

"Apollo," I pleaded, not sure what I was hoping for.

"Boy!" our father's clipped voice barked from the distance.

Apollo backed away slowly before turning and retreating into the woods with the rest of the Reapers. Apollo was the last Reaper to vanish, leaving my family and I in the dark of the forest, settled in a silence that unnerved me. I waited until I knew it was safe and that the Reapers had truly left the woods and weren't hiding in the trees anywhere.

The circle of fire I'd created dissipated and I could feel all my strength leave with it. As the forest went dark again, I collapsed to my knees, the uncontrollable pain that racked my body making me re-aware of the stab wound to my gut. I heard footsteps running toward me as I fell onto my side, feeling the warm blood spill over my fingers at a rapid rate.

I was rolled onto my back and I could feel my head being put into someone's lap as they gently stroked my hair. "Artemis, honey?" Eris's voice pleaded. "Open your eyes for me."

I tried to do what she asked, but I couldn't get my body to cooperate. I felt my eyelids flutter and close again, taking every ounce of strength I had with it.

"Help her!" Eris shouted to someone, but I couldn't see who.

I could feel hands on my stomach and I felt a little warm. "I can heal her, but there's internal damage," Tennessee's voice came from above me.

"Just do something!" Eris's voice shouted hysterically.

"Rhea, I need you to pull the knife out so I can heal her properly, can you do that?" Tennessee asked.

"Yeah," Rhea said, but her voice was rough. "I am so sorry for this, little bird."

I screamed as I felt the pain in my gut worsen, and then finally, it was gone. The shock was so jarring that my eyes snapped opened. My head was in Eris's lap and I saw her tear-stained face look down at me with a little smile.

"Hey there, little bird," she whispered, her voice filled with grief. "Stay with me okay? Just stay here with me."

I looked up beyond her face and could see the canopy of treetops and stars dancing. I smiled a little. "The stars are beautiful tonight," I whispered weakly, unsure that anyone could even hear me.

"That they are, little witch," Tennessee agreed, his face firm as he concentrated on healing the wound. "Just relax and look at the stars. You'll be right as rain in a minute."

My head lolled to the side, and I was looking at Rhode's wolf, who had rested his head near mine so that I could see him clearly. His brown eyes begging me to stay with him, but I didn't know if I could. "It's okay," I breathed, each breath become harder to take in and easier to release.

"Artemis?" Eris asked, confused as if I were rambling.

I kept my eyes on the wolf, unsure if he could understand me, but I had to tell him this. I had to tell them all of this before I just couldn't anymore. "It's okay now, I'm ready," I said weakly.

"Artemis," Eris's voice came closer and her voice was beyond concerned. "Please don't talk like that."

I turned my head slowly to look back up at Eris and smiled. "I love you all," I breathed and my eyes fluttered closed.

"No," Eris voice broke instantly. "Artemis, stay with me. Artemis?"

I didn't have the strength to answer.

"Artemis!"

The last thing I heard before I fell under was Eris's cries echoing through the night, and I could have sworn I heard a wolf howling in the distance.

Chapter 21

I sat up in shock, looking around and seeing myself in a room of all white. I looked down at my stomach and saw the stab wound was gone. No scar. I looked around as I tried to figure out what the hell was going on, and my eyes settled on the blood angel sitting next to me.

"M-Mom?"

She turned to look at me, those beautiful blue eyes of hers shining underneath that halo of blonde hair. "I've missed you, little bird."

I would have started bawling in her arms at that moment, but there was a question that I needed to ask first. "Am I dead?"

She shook her head and reached out to push my hair back from my face. "Not yet, but you need to go back. Go back and take care of your sisters."

"I don't want to go back, Mom," I admitted. "I can't go back to all that fighting and all that hate between the witches and the Reapers."

"You are returning to a war that I prayed you would never have to see, but you are also returning to people that love you more than anything in the world."

"Why didn't you tell me about Apollo?"

"I was hoping that your father would raise him better than with hate in his heart."

"I won't go back just to kill my brother, I won't."

Mom shook her head. "No dear, your destiny isn't death, your destiny is life."

"What are you talking about?"

Mom smiled against and touched my cheek. "Go back, my dear child. I'll see you soon enough."

"Mom?" I asked, confused by what she had just said.

Mom leaned over and kissed my forehead. "Wake up, little bird."

I came back to reality slowly, hearing people talking before anything else clicked into place. I was too weak to move, so I just lay still, listening as the muffled sounds around me became clearer. The voices were something to grab onto, something that I used to help pull me to the surface.

"We're in a motel outside Reno right now," Eris's voice came through. "We're going to spend the night and start driving toward you first thing in the morning. We should get there around dark."

"You should get some sleep," Tennessee's voice came now, but he wasn't talking to me.

"I'm fine," Rhea's voice said. Hers was the closest to me.

"You haven't slept in almost a day, you need sleep."

"I'm fine," Rhea said with more force this time.

"Did you see what she did out there?" Eris asked softly. "Have you ever seen anything like that before in your life?"

"No," Tennessee said evenly.

"No," Rhea breathed, stroking my hair gently. "She has more power than she even realizes, and it's our job to protect her until she can learn to control it."

"I would sacrifice my life for that girl," Tennessee said firmly.

"Don't make promises you can't keep," Rhea said sternly. "Because it just might come to it."

"When I took my Guardian Oath, I swore to protect any witch in my charge. I was sent to protect Artemis, and that is exactly what I will do."

"Eris, what did Izzy say when you called her?" Rhea asked.

"She knows where we are and she's expecting us. She'll give us a safe haven and we can be there while Artemis recuperates."

"Good, the sooner we get her out of this shit and somewhere safe, the better."

"Ray," I sighed her name using all my strength, but it barely came out above a whisper.

The room fell silent and then someone grabbed my hand and squeezed. I tried to open my eyes but could only manage the barest of a second, only enough to see Rhea's face in front of mine, filled with relief.

"Oh, little bird," she sighed. "You scared us there."

"I'm okay," I said, using every ounce of energy I had to speak, but I knew it wouldn't last much longer. I could feel the pain returning and racking my body, stealing the little strength that I have along with it.

"We're all here, Artemis," Eris said gently.

"Rhode?" I breathed.

A warm and reassuring kiss was placed in my hair as finger gently warped around my other hand. "I'm here, darlin'," Rhode whispered. "I'm not going anywhere."

I gave a weak smile, knowing he was there.

"You're safe now," Eris assured me. There was a soft jab on my arm, barely enough for me to notice, and then I was flooded with warmth. "You can rest now."

"I'm scared," I mumbled, my speech slurring a little.

There were the sounds of heavy footsteps coming toward where I was. A kiss was placed gently on my temple. "Sleep now, little witch," Tennessee whispered into my ear. "Sleep deeply and have wonderful dreams. We'll be here when you wake up."

"It hurts," I breathed.

"I know," he said softly, and I could feel the flood of warmth coursing through me take away some of the pain. Not all of it, but enough for me to relax and start to fall back under and slip into a sleep so deep that I didn't dream.

Chapter 22

My eyes opened slowly as my senses came back to me. I was in a bed, but in a bedroom that wasn't mine. None of the things around the room were mine, but all the same, I was certain this was the land of the living. I groaned as light made its way through the room, hurting my already sensitive eyes in very much real world pain.

I shut out the light, trying not to blind myself. I opened my eyes again, slowly this time, letting the light in a little at a time so I could adjust slowly. I was lying on my side, propped up so there wasn't any weight resting on the brand on my back or the stab wound in my stomach.

Rhode was sitting in the chair next to my bed, leaning forward with a book in his hands as he read out loud from it. His eyes flipped up from the book as I guess they did every so often just to look at me. "You're awake," he said, his voice rough from the reading but still the warm tone that made me melt inside.

"Have you been reading to me?" I wasn't even sure that he could hear me because my voice was so weak.

Rhode mouth quirked in a small smile. "Eris said it would help if you heard a familiar voice while you were sleeping."

I sighed, remembering the long afternoons Eris had spent sitting next to me after the accident, reading from books and magazines or just talking to me about anything. Whatever she could do to make me talk, to bring me back to the real world.

"What happened?" I asked in a rough voice, my voice stronger this time as I tried to sit up and immediately regretting that decision as pain ripped through my stomach and side. "Yep, I got stabbed, that part wasn't a dream."

Rhode moved to get out of the chair and I reached out and grabbed his hand frantically, noticing the tubes coming from my arm, but my attention was on Rhode, so I didn't ask about it.

"Hey, hey," Rhode breathed, lowering his lips to my forehead and placing a lingering kiss. "It's okay, I'm just going to tell Eris that you're awake. I'll be right back, I promise."

I nodded slowly, watching anxiously as Rhode went to the door and stuck his head out.

"Eris," he called, "she's awake."

"You found me," I breathed as the memories of the past few days started to come back to me. "Your wolf found me."

Rhode left the door open a crack before he came back to the chair and took his place next to me again. "I promised you that I would find you," he said, his voice serious.

"I know." I smiled. "I never doubted you. Not for a second."

"Good," he said, leaning forward and taking my hand in his, careful not to jostle the needle in my hand. I just stared at him while he linked our fingers, playing with them idly. "We thought we lost you back there for second. You were in and out of it for a little while."

I looked down at the IV in my arm, familiar with the look from my previous experience in hospitals. "Why do I have an IV?"

"You've been asleep almost three days," Rhode said as if it were common knowledge. "We had to make sure you weren't getting dehydrated. Ten's Gift can only do so much and, honestly, he kind of exhausted himself trying to get the bleeding to stop back in the woods."

I nodded, pieces of the forest coming back to me, remembering the knife being pulled out of my gut and Tennessee above me as he tried to heal the wound. "How much could he heal?"

"Ten did his best to heal the stab wound, but there was a lot of internal bleeding that he had to concentrate on. He was able to heal most of the internal damage and get the bleeding to stop, but you'll need to rest and take it easy for a couple of weeks, and there'll be a scar there."

"Better than nothing, I suppose."

Rhode paused for a moment before he added evenly, "I'm afraid there was nothing that Ten could do about the brand on your back, but he managed to help the ribs mend and speed along the healing of the bruises."

I nodded, taking all the information in stride. I could live with the scar on my stomach and brand on my back; hell, I'd wear them as a badge of honor that I escaped from Reapers with my life.

"Knock knock, little bird," Eris said softly as she came into the room. "Glad to hear you're awake."

"Hey, Eris," I smiled softly. "Where are we?"

"At Izzy's."

"We're in Montana?" I asked, a little shocked at all the information coming at me. "Where's Rhea?"

"Sleeping. She wouldn't leave your side since the woods. Had to drug her tea to get her to sleep." Eris motioned Rhode. "Rhode hasn't left your side since we found you. We got him to change back somewhere in Nevada. Guess after what happened, he's still a little over protective."

"It's okay." I smiled, gripping his hand tighter. "Overprotective is a good thing for him." I paused as I felt all my different injuries come together and cause me enough pain to knock an elephant on its ass.

"Are you in pain?" Rhode asked.

I nodded slowly. "Took a bit for my brain to register the pain."

Eris picked up a syringe from the bedside table and leaned over and injected whatever was in the syringe into my IV. "This will help with the pain," she said softly. "It'll most likely knock you out again, but you won't be in any pain. Give it a minute and it'll kick in."

"Wow, it must be really bad if Eris is doling out the good drugs."

"Artemis," Rhode said softly, even though I knew it was meant to chastise me.

"I'll send something up for you to eat when you get up." Eris paused with a frown on her face. "How long has it been? Since they fed you?"

I looked at her but didn't answer, letting the silence speak what we both knew, and I could feel Rhode tense beside me. I brushed my thumb along his hand gently, trying to bring him back from the dark place his mind had gone. "I knew you guys would find me."

"You helped us as well," Eris said gently. "Rhea was right, you have great magic, and now the Reapers know it too."

"Is that a good thing or a bad thing?"

"We'll just have to wait to find out, I suppose."

"I feel warm," I mumbled, my eyes getting heavy, the same warm feeling I had felt back in that hotel room flooding through me. Rhode's hand was wrapped around mine securely, and I felt a peace in that moment.

"That means it's working," Eris said, pulling the covers up and kissing me on the forehead. "Sleep well, little bird."

For once, I actually did.

When I awoke, Tennessee was sitting in the chair this time, reading a book. I lifted my head up to look at him, surprised the pain in my back had subsided substantially from the first time I had woken up.

"Hi," I said softly, noticing that Rhode was no longer lying in the bed next to me.

Tennessee set his book down and looked at me with a smile. "Welcome back, little witch. You gave us quite a scare back there."

"I know, and thank you for healing me. I wouldn't be here without you. Is there water?" I asked, realizing how dry my throat really was.

Tennessee got up and helped me sit up in bed against the headboard before he handed me a glass of water. I drained the entire glass as my thirst from all that time caught up with me. Tennessee took the glass and put it back on the table before he propped up all the pillows on the bed behind me so my back would be comfortable.

Tennessee held out the orange. "I thought you might be hungry."

"I'm starved," I said, taking the orange and peeling it, my mouth watering at the smell of the orange rind tearing away from the fruit.

"I take it that the Reapers didn't take the courtesy to feed you?"

I shook my head. "No, and please don't tell Rhode or my sisters that. They worry enough."

Tennessee nodded. "Your secret if safe with me."

"Where's Rhode?"

It hadn't gone unnoticed by Tennessee that my first thought had been to look for him. "He hasn't left your side in days. I sent him to get something to eat about an hour ago. I think after all that happened he couldn't believe you were really here."

"Yeah, I know the feeling," I said, but Tennessee's eyes weren't on me, they were on my hands which were shaking so violently I couldn't continue to peel my orange.

Tennessee reached out and took the orange from my hand and continued taking up the task for me. "Thank you," he said quietly. "You saved my brother's life by sacrificing yourself, and for that I am forever in your debt." Tennessee finished peeling the orange and placed the peeled fruit in my hand while he kept the rind in his own hand. "You're safe now, Artemis."

"For now, but that won't be the end of it. You and I both know that."

"I will tell you something that few people know. Some spirit witches can see other people's death, my Gift and my curse is that I can see other people's deaths. The when, never the how or the why, but when you called me before you were taken, I no longer saw my brother's death."

"Do you see mine or my sisters' deaths?"

"Even if I did, you know I would never tell you when it would happen, Artemis."

"I know, I just . . . I just want to know if you see theirs. Or if you see mine."

"I've never seen the deaths for either of your sisters. I do, however, see many deaths for you, but I don't know which one it is, if any at all. What I do know is that you are the one that my brother and his wolf have chosen. That means my mission in this life is to protect you, little witch."

"Thank you, Ten."

Tennessee leaned in and kissed my forehead before standing up off the bed. "I'll let Rhea know you're awake. I think she's been the most anxious to see you."

After Tennessee left, I sat on the bed and ate my orange before nature decided to call, loudly. I managed to get myself out of bed and drag myself into the, thankfully adjoining, bathroom, leaning on the IV pole for some support as I wheeled it along with me. Once I was done, I was about to make my way back to the bedroom when I caught a glimpse of myself in the mirror.

My face was still pretty bruised, but I wasn't that surprised considering the beating the Reapers had laid into me. The bruises were starting to lighten up and they'd be gone in a week or two, which was a significant improvement over the healing time of the original wounds. I avoided trying to look at the Reaper's brand on my back; even if I could angle to see it without hurting myself, it wouldn't have done me any good. Instead, I lifted my shirt and saw the tender pink outline of the stab wound that

Apollo made. I reached down and traced it with my fingers, the touch sending a cold shiver through my spine.

"Hey," Rhea's voice came from the door way and I jumped a little. "Sorry, I didn't mean to scare you."

"No." I shook my head. "I'm just a little jumpy is all. My fault."

"You should be in bed resting," Rhea said, not wasting a moment before she became concerned for me and my wellbeing.

I nodded. "I wanted to try and take a shower."

Rhea nodded and did something I rarely saw her do. She conceded. She came into the bathroom and turned on the shower and closed the door as she let the room fill with steam. She took out the IV with more care than I would have ever thought to use and helped me out of my clothes.

"In the tub," she said softly.

I obeyed. Rhea helped me sit down, knowing that I wouldn't be able to stand for long. I sat there quietly and rocked back and forth slowly as Rhea took the detachable shower head and began to wet my hair. Slowly she moved the spray to the rest of my body. "Let me know if anything hurts."

I closed my eyes, falling to the quiet between the two of us as Rhea bathed me, something she hadn't done since I came home a catatonic head case. Even then Rhea hadn't given up on me or let me give up on myself, and she still wouldn't, even now.

There was a tense pause from Rhea, and I knew she was at my back. "How bad is it?" I asked.

"It's bad," she admitted, tracing my back with a gentleness my captors had never thought possible, "but it will heal. You will heal, little bird."

I couldn't hold back the flood gate anymore and I started bawling as I sat there in the tub, unable to stop myself. "I was so scared Ray. I thought I would never see you or Eris again. I thought I was going to die!"

Rhea put her arms around me, rocking with me as she hummed quietly. "Let it out, let it all out."

I did. I sat there and let it all go, crying like a baby as my sister, my protector, held me like I would vanish into thin air.

When I was all cried out, Rhea helped me out of the tub, dried me off and helped me into some clean clothes. I managed to make it back to the bedroom on my own, slowly, but on my own nonetheless. I sat on the bed and looked down at my hands, the same hands that had taken lives.

I was a killer now.

"I don't regret killing them," I said, refusing to look at Rhea. "I don't feel an ounce of guilt for it."

"Good," Rhea said, sinking beside me on the bed, taking my hand into hers. "I was nineteen when I killed my first Reaper."

I looked at her in shock at what she had just said. "You've killed a Reaper?"

Rhea nodded. "Some rookie who had gone rogue and was looking to prove himself. He tried to lure me out of a nightclub. I caught on quick and, once we were in the alley, I slit his throat. Left his body there and made it look like a robbery gone bad. That was the only time I saw a Reaper until that night we found you."

"Why didn't you tell anyone?"

"It didn't seem like a big deal at the time. This was before the Reapers became as numerous as they are, as dangerous. Back when they were just some punks. Now things are different, the Reapers are a threat to us now."

I nodded. "I know."

"Good. I want you to remember that when I'm hard on you, it's because they're dangerous and they will kill us." Rhea leaned over and kissed my forehead. "Izzy's making lunch now, do you need help down the stairs?"

I nodded slowly. "If I walk to the stairs, can you send Rhode up to help me down?"

A knowing smile crossed Rhea's face. "There are some witches that believe spirit witches can become bonded to witches that are meant to be their soul mates. They believe that the bond is strong and for life. Do you love him?"

I took a moment to think about my feelings for Rhode before I answered. "We haven't known each other that long, but I feel something between us, and I feel how strong that pull is. I really like him and yeah, I think one day I will love him."

"All the more reason to fight," Rhea noted before she got up. "I'll send him up. Shout if you need any help."

I took a minute to collect myself before I got up off the bed and started making my way slowly out of the room and down the hallway. By the time I got to the top of the stairs, Rhode was standing there, waiting for me.

The moment he saw me, his eyes went wide and I could tell that he was still a little shocked I was awake after all this time.

"Hey," I said softly.

"Hey," he breathed, reaching out and gently running his thumb along my cheek, caressing the bruises on my face. "Jesus Christ."

"I'm fine," I assured him, reaching up and taking his hand as I leaned into his touch. "Ten helped the healing and I'm going to be just fine." I looked up into those beautiful, toffee-colored eyes of his and smiled. "Thanks to you, I'm going to be just fine."

"Here," Rhode reached into his pocket and pulled out the locket Eris had given me that I left behind at the house when I was taken. "I wanted to wait until you were awake to give it back."

My smile widened as I turned around and swept my head forward, allowing Rhode to put it around my neck. I turned back and leaned in to give him a kiss. "Thank you," I said, our lips still touching. "Come on, let's go have some lunch," I said, grabbing the banister of the stairs as Rhode wrapped his arm around my waist.

"Your cousin is very . . . interesting," Rhode said quietly as we made out decedent.

"Don't worry, she's not by blood, so it doesn't run in the family. Our moms were best friends back in the day and Izzy and I saw each other a lot as kids." I sucked in a quick breath as I stepped down on one of the stairs. I could feel Rhode start to loosen his grip on me but I tightened my grip on him. "Don't you dare let go."

"I don't want to hurt you," he said quietly.

I paused and looked at him. "You're not the reason that I'm hurt, and you're not the reason that I'm hurting now. I'm okay, so please don't treat me like I'm made of glass, I am not going to break."

Rhode nodded and we resumed our journey down the stairs. Once we made it to the bottom, Rhode kept his hand around my waist, allowing me to lean some of my weight against him as I walked into the dining room.

Eris, Rhea, and Tennessee were sitting around the table, all eyes shifting to Rhode and I as we came in, never shifting away as I made slow steps to the table and finally sat down.

"Artemis!" Izzy came into the kitchen, absolutely beaming when she saw me, rushing over to give me a hug. "It's been so long."

"Too long, Iz," I said softly.

"Your sisters told me what happened. Jesus, a fire witch, who've thought?"

"Explains all the fighting at school," I remarked, pushing back Izzy's soft brown hair so that I could better see her hazel eyes and heart shaped face. She hadn't changed since we were twelve. "What's for lunch, cuz?"

"You slept through breakfast, so I thought I'd make a special spread in your honor. We've got eggs, bacon, Belgian waffles, hash browns and sausage. IHOP can eat its heart out."

"Thanks Izzy." I squeezed her hand.

"I'm going to go check on the food, back in two shakes."

Everyone waited for Izzy to go back into the kitchen before anyone spoke. I went first. "I need the agreement that we will talk about this now and then after we enjoy a meal and some real time as a normal family."

"Artemis," Rhea started.

"I just want a couple of days to feel normal again, Ray. Not to feel like some broken and battered witch with some fucking destiny hanging over my head. Can you give me that?"

Rhea nodded. "Yes."

"Then begin," I said quietly. "Tell me everything you know about this prophesy."

Rhea tensed before she spoke. "I was almost eighteen when my magic presented itself. Mom told me about witches and Reapers and everything else that we've told you. The last thing she told me before I moved away was about when you and Apollo were born. She said that she was so nervous about having twins because they might be pitted against one another in the war that was to come."

"That's all she said about it?"

Rhea nodded. "I didn't find out anything else about this until after Mom died. The Elders summoned me and told me about a prophesy of twin witches that were on opposite sides of the war between witches and Reapers. I assured them that you were the only surviving twin. They didn't seem convinced of that, and ever since then I've had a sinking feeling in my stomach that Mom didn't tell us the truth when she said that Apollo had died. That night in the woods only proved what I hoped was wrong."

"So, what happens now that we know Apollo is alive and working within the Reapers?"

"Now we've seen what kind of magic you have. Now you just have to learn now to harness it and control it," Eris said evenly. "Izzy's mentioned that there's a small witch community in the mountains, but she says that fire witches are rare around these parts. So, I'll teach you the basics and we can try to find a fire witch to help you harness your element. Once you've recovered, then we can start."

"Now that we know what we're up against. This isn't going to stop," Rhea said.

"If Apollo has even a fraction of Artemis's magic, then his position among the Reapers will give them a considerable advantage in all of this," Tennessee said, and I felt a shiver go through me as my mind thought back to Apollo. "They won't go down easy. It won't be simple."

"Meaning what, exactly?" Eris asked.

"We prepare," I said softly, taking Rhode's hand in mine. "We prepare for war."

Epilogue

I don't know if I would ever love the night as much as I did before everything changed, before my destiny was laid out before me. The only thing I did know was I had to deal the hand I was dealt in this life and hope for the best.

After everyone was asleep, I snuck out to the front porch and placed a white tea candle on the railing and whispered over it, putting every ounce of hope I had into it. "A call to witches lost, please guide my brother home to his family and protect him from the evil in this life that would wish to hurt him. Lift the hate in his heart and show him the love that has been locked away."

I knelt and blew gently at the wick, concentrating with all my might and smiling when the wick caught fire. I placed the candle in a small lantern and hung it from a hook above the railing.

"Please let this work," I whispered.

"What are you doing out here, darlin'?" Rhode's voice came from behind me, but I didn't turn around to look at him. He approached slowly from behind and placed a blanket around my shoulders as I stood there before turning around and sitting on the railing, staring at me intently. "You haven't even been awake a whole day yet, you should be resting so you can get your strength back."

"I had to do this first," I said softly.

Rhode looked up at the candle glowing in the hanging lantern. "A calling spell," he said softly. "A spell to call for lost witches."

"A spell to call lost witches home," I said firmly.

"You really think that this will bring Apollo back?" he asked. "Even if it did, how do you know that his mind hasn't already been poisoned by your twisted father."

I looked at Rhode and he almost flinched when he saw the tears gleaming in my eyes. "I don't know," I breathed. "What I do know is that my mother raised my sisters and we protect each other. That's what I'm doing. I'm protecting my little brother, and I'm protecting my siblings, my family from that twisted man that would see us dead."

"Such courage," he said quietly.

"I don't know what's going to happen next, but I need to make sure that I try and make everything right. If you're not going to help me do that, then I free you from your role as my Guardian."

"My dear Artemis." Rhode breathed, standing up off the railing and coming closer to me until we had only an inch of space between our bodies. He placed his index finger under my chin and gently tilted my head up to look into his eyes. "I would have thought that at this point it was obvious that I would walk through hell and back for you. I am always in your corner, no matter your decision; there's no breaking the connection we have."

"Good," I whispered, leaning in so that my lips brushed his, "because there's this guy that I really like."

"Oh?" he asked, his eyebrow quirking up.

"Yeah. He's my best friend, but I don't want to complicate anything. What should I do?"

"I think you should follow your heart, darlin'."

I smiled at that answer. Plus, I really loved it when he called me darlin', all long and drawn out with that accent making the word sound like a poem. "Good," I said, leaning in and kissing him.

He kissed me back and we fell into each other, unconcerned about what the future would hold at the moment. In that time and in that space, we were just two crazy teenagers head over heels about each other.

In that moment, I couldn't have been happier.

Printed in the United States
By Bookmasters